初级上

LOVE CHINESE AT FIRST SIGHT

Primary Level

施洁民 [日] 蒲丰彦 编著
范祥涛 译

一见钟情学汉语

(英语版)

上海译文出版社

Table of Contents

Preface

Learning Chinese at First Sight is a textbook written for beginners of Chinese learning in English countries. It includes four volumes: Primary Level (Vols. I, II) and Intermediate Level (Vols. I, II).

In recent years with the constant intensification of communication between China and English countries in various fields, there have been an increasing number of people from these countries to come to China for study or visit or both. More enterprises from English countries choose to invest in China. These students, visitors and people from these countries staying at or living permanently in China for the sake of work — all of them highly expect to learn Chinese in a short period of time, using correct pronunciation to exchange ideas with Chinese people and correct speech to work. *Learning Chinese at First Sight* is a textbook just intended to satisfy these needs. For the convenience of beginners to remember what is learned, many exercises are specially designed.

This book is the first volume of the Primary Level, including such two parts as pronunciation and texts, in which over 670 words and more than 60 sentence patterns are embraced. They are mostly selected respectively from the contents of the first and second levels in *The Outline of HSK Vocabulary* and *The Outline of HSK Grammar*. Moreover, tens of new words are added which have been internalized in real life.

Our sincere thanks are indebted to Mr. Shen Xunfeng from Shanghai Translation Publishing House for his kind instructions during the writing and publication of this book.

Compiler
June, 2003

词性简称表
Abbreviations

adj.	adjective	形容词
adv.	adverb	副词
aux.	auxiliary	助动词
cl.	classifier	量词
conj.	conjunction	连词
int.	interjection	叹词
n.	noun	名词
num.	numeral	数词
pref.	prefix	词头
prep.	preposition	介词
pron.	pronoun	代词
suf.	suffix	词尾
v.	verb	动词

Pronunciation

Chinese pronunciation consists of initials and finals in addition to four tones. Initials are similar to consonants and finals to vowels in English.

I. Finals

1. Monophthongs

Chinese pronunciation system has seven basic monophthongs in total. They are

a o e i u ü er

The pronunciation of /**ɑ**/ is similar to the English vowel /**a:**/, with the mouth open widest and the tongue lowest in the mouth among all vowels.

The final /**o**/ is pronounced with the mouth rounded and smaller than when pronouncing /**ɑ**/. It is similar to the short vowel /**u**/ in the word "book", but the mouth is rounded and bigger in pronouncing /**o**/.

The Chinese sound /**e**/ differs considerably from any one in English. Its pronunciation is closer to the English sound /ə:/, but the former is pronounced with an obstruction between the back of the tongue and the soft palate.

The Chinese sounds /**i**/ and /**u**/ are similar to /**i**/ and /**u:**/ in English. But in pronouncing /**i**/, there is an obstruction between the front of the tongue and the front of the hard palate. Due to the influence of English pronunciation, some people tend to mispronounce the Chinese sound /**i**/ as the English vowel /**i**/.

The Chinese final /**ü**/ has no similar sound in English. It is pronounced in a manner similar to the English sound /**u:**/, but with the front of the tongue higher and an obstruction between the front of the tongue and the front of the hard palate.

The Chinese final /**er**/ is pronounced with the tip of the tongue curled back, but not touching the hard palate. So it is similar to the English consonant /**r**/.

2. Compound finals

In Chinese, there are frequently the cases where two or three monophthongs are combined to form compound finals, including diphthongs, which can also be found in English. There are 13 of them in Chinese as follows.

ai	ei	ao	ou	
ia	ie	ua	uo	üe
iao	iou	uai	uei	

These compound finals fall into the falling categories:

① Diphthongs

Diphthongs are finals which include two monophthongs, such as /**ai**/, /**ei**/, /**ao**/, /**ou**/, /**ia**/, /**ie**/, /**ua**/, /**uo**/, and /**üe**/. They are pronounced by sliding from one sound to another. But in reading these diphthongs, the two parts within each cannot be distinctively separated. This is similar to the pronunciation of diphthongs in English.

The pronunciation of compound finals with the vowel /**e**/ is comparatively complex. There are four of them:

ei	ie	üe	uei

They are pronounced with a variation because of the influence of another sound in the same compound final. For example, in spite of the pronunciation of /**e**/, the Chinese sound /**ie**/ is pronounced in a manner similar to /**je**/, and the Chinese sound /**ei**/ is similar to /**ei**/ in English.

② Compound finals with three monophthongs

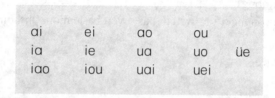

There are four compound finals in Chinese which have three monophthongs. They are /**iao**/, /**iou**/, /**uai**/, and /**uei**/. Here /**u**/ is similar to the English consonant /**w**/ and /**i**/ similar to /**j**/. So in reading these compound finals, it is necessary to read all the three sounds without any separation.

③ Nasal compound finals

In Chinese there are those finals ending with nasal consonants /**n**/ and /**ng**/, which have pronunciation respectively similar to /**n**/ and /ŋ/ in English. The following are such nasal compound finals and their roughly corresponding English pronunciations.

Chinese	an	ang	en	eng	in	ing	ong
English	æn	aːŋ	ən	əŋ	in	iŋ	ɔŋ

Besides, there are other nasal compound finals which combine more finals with /**n**/ and /**ng**/, such as /**ian**/, /**iang**/, /**uan**/, /**uang**/, /**uen**/, /**ueng**/ and /**iong**/. Here again both /**i**/ and /**u**/ are respectively similar to /**j**/ and /**w**/ in English.

Chinese	ian	iang	uan	uang	uen	ueng	iong
English	jæn	jaːŋ	wæn	waːŋ	wən	wəŋ	jɔŋ

Another two nasal compound vowels in Chinese are /**üan**/ and /**ün**/, which are similar to /**juæn**/ and /**jun**/ respectively in English.

In pronouncing a compound final all sounds within it must be read smoothly. Moreover, there are some sounds which have to be imitated after native speakers since their pronunciations are hard to be described exactly.

II. Initials

Chinese pronunciation system has 23 initials, some of which roughly correspond to the consonants in English, as is shown in the following table.

Chinese	English	Chinese	English	Chinese	English	Chinese	English
b	b	p	p	m	m	f	f
d	d	t	t	n	n	l	l
g	g	k	k	h	h		
j	dʒi	q	tʃi	x	ʃi	r	r
zh		ch		sh		w	w
z	dz	c	ts	s	s	y	j

Among the above 23 Chinese initials, some are pronounced roughly in the same way as those corresponding ones in English while the others have pronunciations different from those in English.

Three points deserve special attention in practicing their pronunciations:

(1) Pronunciations of initials;

(2) Sounds which English pronunciation system does not have;

(3) The place and manner of obstruction.

The pronunciations of Chinese consonants will be explained in detail in the following.

1. Pronunciation of initials

①Initials similar to those in English

The Chinese language adopts Latin letters to indicate its pronunciation. Therefore, some Chinese initials are pronounced in ways similar to those English ones, as are shown in the above table.

For example, /**mɑ**/ in Chinese is pronounced as /**ma:**/ in English.

②Initials different from those in English

The Chinese sound /**g**/ is pronounced as /**g**/ instead of /**dʒi:**/, /**j**/ as /**dʒi:**/ instead of /**j**/, /**q**/ as /**tʃi:**/ instead of /**kju:**/, /**x**/ as /**ʃi**/ instead of /**eks**/, /**z**/ as /**dz**/ instead of /**zi:**/ or /**zed**/, /**c**/ as /**ts**/ instead of /**si:**/, and /**y**/ as /**j**/ instead of /**wai**/.

The Chinese initial /**h**/ actually is pronounced a little differently in comparison with the glottal /**h**/ in English. The pronunciation of the former has an obstruction between the back of the tongue and the soft palate, and a scraping noise is made at that point, while the obstruction in pronouncing the latter is at the glottis, and there is less obstruction at that point.

2. Non-corresponding sounds

In Chinese initials there are still three sounds, i. e. /**zh**/, /**ch**/ and /**sh**/, which are pronounced in special ways and have no corresponding sounds in English. Beginners need to imitate after teachers in order to pronounce them accurately. Furthermore, the Chinese language does not have the English consonant /**v**/, for which /**w**/ is used instead.

The sounds /**zh**/, /**ch**/ and /**sh**/ are most difficult to pronounce in Chinese. In pronouncing them, the tongue is curved, the tip of the tongue is close to the upper teeth ridge and light friction is made to produce these sounds.

3. The place and manner of obstruction

All Chinese initials are aspirated and voiced in their pronunciation, because they are read by combining them with another Chinese vowel, as are shown in the following table. So there is a further distinction between the sound values and their readings.

initial	reading	initial	reading	initial	reading	initial	reading
b	bo	p	po	m	mo	f	fe
d	de	t	te	n	ne	l	le
g	ge	k	ke	h	he		
j	ji	q	qi	x	xi	r	ri
zh	zhi	ch	chi	sh	shi	w	wa
z	zi	c	ci	s	si	y	ya

It is clear from the above table that the reading of a Chinese initial is always combined with another final, which is different from the reading of consonants in English. The reading of Chinese initials remains the same when they combine with another final or finals to indicate the reading of a Chinese character. So the reading of a Chinese character has three parts. For instance, the reading "b + ɑ" is "b + o + ɑ", but the final reading is still "bɑ".

According to the place of obstruction and manner of obstruction, Chinese initials fall into seven groups:

(1) bi-labial — /**b**/, /**p**/, and /**m**/, where the obstruction is formed by the two lips;

(2) labiodental — /**f**/, where the obstruction is formed between the upper teeth and lower lip;

(3) alveolar — /**d**/, /**t**/, /**n**/, and /**l**/, where the obstruction is formed by the tip of the tongue and the upper teeth ridge;

(4) retroflex — /**zh**/, /**ch**/, /**sh**/, and /**r**/, where the obstruction is formed by the tip of the tongue and the back of the teeth ridge;

(5) palato-alveolar — /**j**/, /**q**/, and /**x**/, where the obstruction is formed between the surface of tip of the tongue and the teeth ridge;

(6) alveolar — /**z**/, /**c**/, and /**s**/, where the obstruction is formed between the tip of the tongue and the inside of the upper teeth;

(7) velar — /**g**/, /**k**/, and /**h**/, where the obstruction is formed between the back of the tongue and the soft palate

III. Special pronunciations

In Chinese pronunciation, it is only needed to combine initials with finals to read Chinese characters. But there are some special pronunciations which do not conform to this way of reading.

①Changes in reading "initial + final"

In pronouncing "initial + uei", the sound /**e**/ becomes weak and will be omitted, so /**uei**/ is read as /**ui**/, as in /**dui**/, /**gui**/, etc. Similarly, /**iou**/ is read as /**iu**/, as in /**diu**/, /**tiu**/, etc., and /**uen**/ as /**un**/, as in /**dun**/, /**gun**/, etc.

②/**zi**/, /**ci**/ and /**si**/

The sound /**i**/ in Chinese is similar to /**i**/ in English. Therefore it is possible to pronounce /**zi**/, /**ci**/ and /**si**/ as /**dzi**/, /**tsi**/ and /**si**/. In fact, the sound /**i**/ in /**zi**/, /**ci**/ and /**si**/ is not pronounced as /**i**/, but with some modifications. As a result, /**zi**/, /**ci**/ and /**si**/ are respectively pronounced as /**dz**/, /**ts**/, and /**s**/, omitting the final /**i**/.

③iɑn

The Chinese final /**ɑ**/ is similar to the English vowel /**a:**/. But in pronouncing /**iɑn**/, the sound /**ɑ**/ between /**i**/ and /**n**/ is similar to another English sound /**æ**/. Then /**iɑn**/ should be pronounced as /**iæn**/, as in /**jiɑn**/ and /**tiɑn**/, which are respectively pronounced as /**dʒiæn**/ and /**tiæn**/. But there is no change in pronouncing /**jiɑng**/, which is pronounced as /**dʒiaŋ**/.

Besides there are two principles for writing Chinese *pinyin*, as follows:

①When Chinese finals begin with /**i**/ or /**u**/ where there are no initials to combine with them, then /**i**/ will be changed as /**y**/ and /**u**/ into /**w**/. That is, /**i**/, /**iɑ**/ /**iɑo**/... should be changed as /**yi**/, /**yɑ**/, /**yɑo**/... and /**u**/, /**uɑ**/, /**uo**/... should be changed as /**wu**/, /**wɑ**/, /**wo**/...

②When /**j**/, /**q**/, and /**x**/ are followed by the Chinese final /**ü**/, /**ü**/ will be written as /**u**/, as in /**ju**/, /**que**/, /**xuɑn**/..., respectively for /**jü**/, /**qüe**/, /**xüɑn**/. This is because the consonants /**j**/, /**q**/ and /**x**/ are never used together with the final /**u**/ in Chinese.

IV. Four tones

1. Four tones and their positions

The pronunciation of a Chinese character generally consists of three parts: initial, final, and tone. For example, in pronouncing the Chinese characters "中国", only /**zhong**/ and /**guo**/ are incomplete. With the addition of tones, they will become /**zhōngguó**/, which are complete *pinyin* for these two characters. There are four types of tone in modern standard Chinese pronunciation, called "four tones".

(1)The first tone, called "level tone" and marked as "ˉ", which is high and long in pronunciation, as in /**kāi**/, /**gē**/, etc.

(2)The second tone, called "rising tone" and marked as "ˊ", which rises from a modest tone to the higher "level tone", as in /**dí**/, /**gé**/, etc.

(3) The third tone, called "falling-rising tone" and marked as " ˇ ", which first falls from a modest tone and then rises, but the rising part is normally not pronounced, as in /**kǎi**/, /**gǔ**/, etc.

(4) The fourth tone, called "falling tone" and marked as " ˋ ", which falls considerably from the level tone, as in /**dà**/, /**gù**/, etc.

Generally, one of these tone marks is placed on the top of a final in the pronunciation of a Chinese character. If there are two or more finals in a syllable, the tone mark is placed on the top of one final in such an order as /**ɑ**/, /**o**/, /**e**/, /**i**/, /**u**/ and /**ü**/. For example, in the syllable /**lɑi**/, the tone mark is placed on the top of /**ɑ**/, with the result of /**lái**/; in the pronunciation /**shui**/, the tone mark is placed on the top of /**i**/, with the result of /**shuǐ**/.

There is one exception in this principle. When there is the diphthong /**iü**/, the tone mark is placed on the top of /**ü**/ rather than /**i**/, as in /**xiū**/, /**liǔ**/, etc.

2. Tone Sandhi

Each Chinese character generally has one fixed tone. But in a small number of instances this fixed tone may change as a result of the influence from the tones before and after it.

(1) Two 3rd tones in a row

When the third tone occurs continuously, the tone changes in the following way:

third tone + third tone → second tone + third tone

For example, when /**ěr**/ and /**qiě**/ occur together, they are pronounced as /**érqiě**/ instead of /**ěrqiě**/.

(2) Rule for /**bù**/

The Chinese character /**bù**/ for negation changes from the fourth tone to the second tone when it occurs together with a fourth tone. For example, when /**bù**/ and /**bì**/ occur together, they are pronounced as /**búbì**/ instead of /**bùbì**/.

(3) Rules for /**yī**/

① The pronunciation of /**yī**/ (meaning "one") has the first tone. But when it is followed by the first, second, or third tone, it changes into the fourth tone. For example, /**yī**/ and /**biān**/ put together should be pronounced as /**yìbiān**/; /**yī**/ and /**rén**/ put together should be pronounced as /**yìrén**/; /**yī**/ and /**běn**/ put together should be pronounced as /**yìběn**/.

②When /**yī**/ occurs with the fourth tone, it changes into the second tone. For example, /**yī**/ and /**bàn**/ put together should be pronounced as /**yíbàn**/.

③ It remains unchanged when it indicates order or when it is in isolation and directly pronounced.

3. Neutral Tone

Besides the four tones, there are occasions where no tone mark is used in pronouncing some Chinese characters. These characters are usually used as suffixes after another character, such as /**zǐ**/, /**tóu**/. For example, /**hái**/ and /**zǐ**/ put together should be pronounced as /**háizi**/ (meaning "children") instead of /**háizǐ**/; /**shí**/ and /**tóu**/ put together should be pronounced as /**shítou**/ (meaning "stone") instead of /**shítóu**/.

In modern Chinese pronunciation, neutral tone is not confined to the pronunciation of these suffixes. It is also used in pronouncing a Chinese expression consisting of two characters, where the second one may be pronounced with a neutral tone. For example, /**dì**/ and /**fāng**/ put together should be pronounced as /**dìfang**/ with the meaning of "place"; /**luóbo**/ is a fixed expression which means "radish" in English. Neutral tone in reading characters results from habit. More examples:

谢谢 xièxie　　对不起 duìbuqǐ

先生 xiānsheng　　小姐 xiǎojie

4. The retroflex sound /er/

This refers to the Chinese suffix /**er**/, as in /**huār**/ (flower). It is pronounced with the tongue curved backward and it is similar to the sound /**r**/ in the word "door", which is articulated in American English.

In the cases of Chinese words with the ending of /**i**/ or /**n**/, they are pronounced with some changes. For example, /**cí**/ followed by /**er**/ should be pronounced as /**cér**/. For more examples,

小孩儿 xiǎoháir　　玩儿 wánr

The following cases deserve special attention：

(1)The meanings of words are changed when /**er**/ is added. For example，some words are changed to indicate places when /**er**/ is added to them. The Chinese character "眼" /**yǎn**/ means "eye", but its meaning is changed into "hole" when this character is followed by /**er**/. More examples，

这(this)→这儿(here)　　那(that)→那儿(there)

(2)The parts of speech are changed when /**er**/ is added. The Chinese character "尖" /**jiān**/ is an adjective which means "sharp", but it is changed into a noun with the meaning of "tip" when it is followed by /**er**/. More examples，

画(v.)→画儿(n.)　　弯(adj.)→弯儿(n.)

(3)In some cases，there is no necessity to use the sound /**er**/ after the Chinese characters. When this sound is deliberately used，the resulting words can get new shades of meaning：friendliness，loveliness，buoyancy，etc. For example，the Chinese word "金鱼" (/**jīnyǘ**/, meaning "goldfish") may be followed by /**er**/ to express the speaker's love for goldfish. More examples，

猫儿(māor)　　鸟儿(niǎor)　　玩儿(wánr)　　花儿(huār)

(4) Words with the suffix of /**er**/ may be changed into different words. For example，

一块(num. + classifier) →一快儿(adv. together)

一点(num. + classifier) →一点儿(n. a little)

【Chinese Pronu

finals / initials	)							Medial (ü)			
	a	o		ıan	uen -un	uang	ueng	ü	üe	üan	ün
b	ba	bo									
p	pa	po									
m	ma	mo	r								
f	fa	fo									
d	da			uan	dun						
t	ta			uan	tun						
n	na			uan				nü	nüe		
l	la	lo		uan	lun			lü	lüe		
g	ga			uan	gun	guang					
k	ka			uan	kun	kuang					
h	ha			uan	hun	huang					
j								ju	jue	juan	jun
q								qu	que	quan	qun
x								xu	xue	xuan	xun
zh	zha			zuan	zhun	zhuang					
ch	cha			cuan	chun	chuang					
sh	sha			suan	shun	shuang					
r				uan	run						
z	za			uan	zun						
c	ca			uan	cun						
s	sa			uan	sun						
	a	o		an	wen	wang	weng	yu	yue	yuan	yun

Dì yī kè

第一课

Wǒ shì zhùwàirényuán

我 是 驻外人员

Language Points

a. 我是约翰·史密斯。

b. 我不是学生。

c. 他是中国人吗？

Text

Nín hǎo! Wǒ shì Shǐmìsī, shì Měiguó zhùwàirényuán.
史密斯：您好！我是史密斯，是美国驻外人员。

Nín hǎo! Wǒ xìng Wáng. Tā xìng Jiāng.
王小姐：您好！我姓王。他姓江。

Jiāng xiānsheng, nín hǎo!
史密斯：江先生，您好！

Nín hǎo, Shǐmìsī xiānsheng!
江先生：您好，史密斯先生！

Qǐng zuò!
王小姐：请坐！

Xièxie!
史密斯：谢谢！

Words

1. 我	wǒ	(pron.)	I
2. 是	shì	(v.)	be, is, am, are
3. 不	bù	(adv.)	not
4. 学生	xuésheng	(n.)	student
5. 他	tā	(pron.)	he
6. 人	rén	(n.)	person
7. 吗	ma	(aux.)	(indicating a question)
8. 驻外人员	zhùwàirényuán	(n.)	person living abroad
9. 你	nǐ	(pron.)	you
10. 您	nín	(pron.)	(honorific form of "你")
11. 好	hǎo	(adj.)	good
12. 姓	xìng	(v.)	... surname is ...
13. 先生	xiānsheng	(n.)	Mr.
14. 小姐	xiǎojie	(n.)	miss
15. 请	qǐng	(v.)	please

16. 坐	zuò	(v.)	sit
17. 谢谢	xièxie	(v.)	thank

Proper nouns

(一)

1. 约翰·史密斯 Yuēhàn Shǐmìsī
2. 江兴 Jiāng Xìng
3. 王丽丽 Wáng Lìli
4. 张颖 Zhāng Yǐng

(二)

1. 中国 Zhōngguó
2. 美国 Měiguó
3. 上海 Shànghǎi

Supplementary words

1. 留学生	liúxuéshēng	(n.)	student studying abroad
2. 公司	gōngsī	(n.)	company
3. 职员	zhíyuán	(n.)	employee
4. 老师	lǎoshī	(n.)	teacher
5. 办事员	bànshìyuán	(n.)	clerk
6. 总经理	zǒngjīnglǐ	(n.)	general manager
7. 技术员	jìshùyuán	(n.)	technician
8. 秘书	mìshū	(n.)	secretary
9. 她	tā	(pron.)	she
10. 叫	jiào	(v.)	call
11. 谁	shuí	(pron.)	who
12. 什么	shénme	(pron.)	what
13. 们	men	(suffix.)	(indicating a plural form)
14. 都	dōu	(adv.)	all
15. 校长	xiàozhǎng	(n.)	president

Grammatical explanation

一、"是" and the form of its negation

In a statement explaining "... (subject) is ... (what)", it is not necessary to use "是" between the subject and the following part. But in explaining the state or action, it is not necessary to use "是". A sentence with the Chinese character "是" is called a sentence of judgment. In a negative sentence, the negation word "不" is used. For example:

(1)史密斯是美国人。 (Smith is an American.)
(2)她不是美国人。 (She is not an American.)
(3)他是总经理。 (He is a general manager.)
(4)张小姐不是老师。 (Miss Zhang is not a teacher.)

二、Interrogative sentence and "吗" (indicating mood of question)

In the Chinese language, an interrogative sentence may end with some characters indicating mood of question. Characters of this kind include "吗", "呢", etc. They have no counterparts in the English language, where the word order is changed and a question mark is used for the same function. For example:

(1)他是张校长吗? (Is he President Zhang?)
(2)你是学生吗? (Are you a student?)

三、The distinction between "姓" and "叫"

Both "姓" and "叫" serve to introduce a person, telling the listeners of the surname or full name of this person. They differ in that the former only involves the family name while the latter is concerned with the full name. For example:

(1)我姓史密斯。 (My family name is Smith.)
(2)我叫约翰·史密斯。(My name is John Smith.)

四、"先生"

This Chinese expression is normally used to address a male person though it can also be used to address a female person. For example:

(1)江先生是中国人。 (Mr. Jiang is a Chinese.)

It is also used to refer to the husband of a couple. For example:

(1)我先生是总经理。 (My husband is a general manager.)

In addressing a young female, another expression "小姐" is used, while in addressing an adult female, "女士" is used. For example:

(1)张小姐 (Miss Zhang) (2)王小姐(Miss Wang)

Exercise I

Please read aloud the following sentences.

1. ① 你好！我是史密斯，是美国驻外人员。
   ② 你好！我是江兴，是公司职员。
   ③ 你好！我是秘书。
   ④ 你好！我是中国人。
   ⑤ 你好！我是美国人。

2. ① 您好！我姓王。
   ② 您好！我姓江。
   ③ 您好！我姓史密斯。
   ④ 您好！我叫约翰·史密斯。
   ⑤ 您好！我叫江兴。

3. 例：我是中国人。→ 我不是中国人。
   ① 他是上海人。
   ② 史密斯先生是留学生。
   ③ 我是公司职员。
   ④ 王小姐是老师。
   ⑤ 她是美国人。

4. 例：你是美国人吗？→ 是，我是美国人。
   ① 你是办事员吗？
   ② 他是总经理吗？
   ③ 史密斯先生是驻外人员吗？
   ④ 张小姐是技术员吗？
   ⑤ 她是秘书吗？

5. 例：他是美国人吗？→ 不是，他不是美国人。
   ① 他是办事员吗？
   ② 你是总经理吗？
   ③ 她是驻外人员吗？
   ④ 江先生是技术员吗？
   ⑤ 王小姐是秘书吗？

6. 例：他们都是美国人吗？→ 是，他们都是美国人。
   ① 你们都是公司职员吗？
   ② 他们都是技术员吗？
   ③ 她们都是留学生吗？

Exercise II

Please practice reading the following dialogues.

1. A：你好！我叫张颖。
   B：我叫约翰·史密斯。你好！
   ① 江兴　　② 王丽丽

2. A：您姓什么？
   B：我姓江。
   ①张　　②史密斯

3. A：他是谁？
   B：他是驻外人员。
   ① 技术员　　② 总经理

4. A：谁是留学生？
   B：她是留学生。
   ①我　　②他

Assignment I

Please translate the following sentences into Chinese and read them aloud.

1. My family name is Zhang.
2. He is Li Dawei. He is a person living abroad.
3. Who is she?
4. Mr. Wang is a secretary.
5. Mr.（Miss）Zhang is not a teacher.
6. Is he a student studying abroad?
7. We are all Chinese.

8. They are all Shanghai natives.

Assignment II

Please use your own background to complete the following dialogues.

1. A：你好！我姓________________。

   B：你好！我姓王。

2. A：您叫什么？

   B：__________________________。

3. A：你是中国人吗？

   B：__________，我__________________________。

4. A：您是公司职员吗？

   B：______________________________。

5. A：你是秘书吗？

   B：__________，___________________________。

Dì èr kè

第二课

Zhè shì nín de yàoshi

这 是 您 的 钥匙

Language Points

a. 这是手机。
b. 这是我的手机。
c. 这个也是我的。
d. 那个是不是他的？

Text

Qǐng wèn, nǎ wèi shì guǎnlǐyuán?
史密斯：请问，哪位是管理员？

Wǒ shì guǎnlǐyuán.
公寓管理员：我是管理员。

Wǒ shì Měiguó ruǎnjiàn gōngsī de Shǐmìsī.
史密斯：我是美国软件公司的史密斯。

Nín jiùshì Shǐmìsī xiānsheng ma? Nín hǎo!
公寓管理员：您就是史密斯先生吗？您好！

Nín hǎo!
史密斯：您好！

Nín de fángjiān shì shíyī lóu sìshíbā shì,
公寓管理员：您的房间是11楼48室，
zhè shì nín de fángjiān yàoshi.
这是您的房间钥匙。

Xièxie!
史密斯：谢谢！

Words

1.	这	zhè	(pron.)	this
2.	手机	shǒujī	(n.)	cell phone, mobile phone
3.	的	de	(aux.)	of
4.	这个	zhège	(pron.)	this
5.	也	yě	(adv.)	also
6.	钥匙	yàoshi	(n.)	key
7.	请问	qǐngwèn		Would you please tell me ...?
8.	哪	nǎ	(pron.)	which
9.	位	wèi	(cl.)	(honorific form)
10.	管理员	guǎnlǐyuán	(n.)	administrator
11.	软件	ruǎnjiàn	(n.)	software

12. 就	jiù	(adv.)	(for emphasis)
13. 房间	fángjiān	(n.)	room
14. 楼	lóu	(n.)	building
15. 室	shì	(n.)	room
16. 公寓	gōngyù	(n.)	boarding house

Proper nouns

1. 布朗	Bùlǎng
2. 周	Zhōu
3. 黄	Huáng
4. 林达	Líndá
5. 杰夫	Jiéfū

Supplementary words

1. 手表	shǒubiǎo	(n.)	watch
2. 电话卡	diànhuàkǎ	(n.)	IC card, smart card
3. 书	shū	(n.)	book
4. 铅笔	qiānbǐ	(n.)	pencil
5. 衣服	yīfu	(n.)	clothes
6. 块	kuài	(cl.)	piece, cake, loaf
7. 张	zhāng	(cl.)	piece, sheet
8. 本	běn	(cl.)	(of book)
9. 支	zhī	(cl.)	(of things with a shape of stick)
10. 件	jiàn	(cl.)	piece (of clothes)
11. 本子	běnzi	(n.)	notebook
12. 信	xìn	(n.)	letter
13. 词典	cídiǎn	(n.)	dictionary
14. 汉语	Hànyǔ	(n.)	Chinese
15. 美国	Měiguó	(n.)	America
16. 英语	Yīngyǔ	(n.)	English
英文	Yīngwén		
17. 那个	nàge	(pron.)	that
18. 把	bǎ	(cl.)	(used of things with a handle)

19. 伞	sǎn	(n.)	umbrella
20. 部	bù	(cl.)	(used of cell phones, etc)

Grammatical explanation

一、Demonstrative pronouns and their plural forms

Chinese language has such demonstrative pronouns as "这", "那" and "哪". Their plural forms are respectively "这些", "那些", and "哪些".

In Chinese a classifier should be added between a demonstrative pronoun and the noun after it. For example:

(1)这本书　(this book)
(2)那件衣服　(that piece of clothes)
(3)这部手机　(that cell phone)
(4)那位管理员　(that administrator)

For a thing or person nearby the demonstrative pronoun "这" is used while for a thing or a person in the distance the demonstrative pronoun "那" is used.

The noun after the demonstrative pronoun can be omitted and we can use the structure "demonstrative pronoun + classifier" independently, such as "这本" and "这个".

Such English expressions as "which book" and "which clothes" should be as follows in Chinese:

(1)哪本书　(which book)
(2)哪件衣服　(which clothes)

The plural forms of Chinese demonstrative pronouns are formed by replacing the classifier by the Chinese character "些". For example:

(1)这些书　(these books)
(2)那些衣服　(those clothes)

this	that	which
这	那	哪
这个	那个	哪个
这本	那本	哪本
这些	那些	哪些

二、“这是”and“这个是”

The Chinese demonstrative pronouns “这” and “那” are generally not used in isolation，but used in such expressions as “这个”(zhègè, this) or “那个”（nàgè，that). However，such structures as “这是～” and“那是～” are exceptions.

(1)这是钥匙。 (This is a key.)

(2)那是书。 (That is a book.)

It is also possible to use the demonstrative pronouns in the following way,

(1)这个是钥匙。 (This is a key.)

(2)那些是书。 (Those are books.)

三、“也”

The Chinese character “也”(yě) has the meaning of “also”.

(1)我是美国人,她也是美国人。

(I am an American and she is also an American.)

(2)这是汉语书,那也是汉语书。

(This is a Chinese book and that is also a Chinese book.)

四、“的”

The Chinese character “的”(de) indicates possession，roughly corresponding to the English preposition “of”.

(1)我们的钥匙 (our key)

(2)你的手表 (your watch)

(3)美国公司的史密斯先生 (Mr. Smith of the American company)

The nouns after “的” can be omitted，as in the following examples.

(1)这张电话卡是黄先生的。 (This IC card is Mr. Huáng's.)
(2)这支铅笔是你的吗? (Is this pencil yours?)

五、"就 + 是"

The Chinese character "就" is generally used for emphasis with the meanings of "no other than" or "only".

(1)这不是我的,那就是我的。 (This is not mine. Only that is mine.)
(2)她就是我们公司的总经理。(She is the very general manager of our company.)

六、"是不是" as a structure for question

The simplest form of a question in Chinese is to add the question particle "吗" at the end of a sentence. In addition, the negative form of "是不是" can also be a question, which has a meaning similar to the structure "…吗?".

(1)这本词典是不是你的? (Is this dictionary yours?)
(2)他是不是中国人? (Is he a Chinese?)

A variation of the structure "是不是" is "…是…不是". Both structures have the same meaning.

(1)这本词典是你的不是? (Is this dictionary yours?)
(2)他是中国人不是? (Is he a Chinese?)

Exercise I

Please read aloud the following sentences.

1. ① 您就是杰夫先生吗?
   ② 你就是美国留学生吗?
   ③ 您就是总经理吗?
   ④ 你就是王小姐吗?
   ⑤ 您就是江先生吗?

2. ① 这是您的房间钥匙。
   ② 这是您的手机。
   ③ 那是他的书。

④ 那是我的衣服。
⑤ 这是她的本子。

3. 例：这是你的手机吗？→ 是的，这是我的手机。
① 这是布朗小姐的手表吗？
② 这是周先生的电话卡吗？
③ 那是黄老师的书吗？
④ 那是你的铅笔吗？
⑤ 这是她的衣服吗？

4. 例：这也是你的手机吗？→ 是的，这也是我的手机。
① 这也是布朗小姐的手表吗？
② 这也是周先生的电话卡吗？
③ 那也是黄老师的书吗？
④ 那也是你的铅笔吗？
⑤ 这也是她的衣服吗？

5. 例：这部手机是你的吗？→ 不是，这部手机不是我的。
① 这块手表是你的吗？
② 那张电话卡是她的吗？
③ 这本书是你的吗？
④ 那支铅笔是王小姐的吗？
⑤ 那件衣服是江先生的吗？

6. 例：这是不是你的手机？→ 是的，这是我的手机。
这是不是你的手机？→ 不是，这不是我的手机。
① 这是不是你的手表？
② 那是不是她的电话卡？
③ 这是不是你的书？
④ 那是不是王小姐的铅笔？
⑤ 那是不是江先生的衣服？

Exercise II

Please practice reading the following dialogues.

1. A：这是什么？
   B：这是本子。
   ① 信　　② 词典

2. A：这是什么书？
   B：这是汉语书。
   ① 日语　　② 英语

3. A：这个是谁的？
   B：是史密斯小姐的。
   A：那个也是她的吗？
   B：不是，那个是我的。
   ① 林达　　② 张

4. A：这把钥匙是谁的？
   B：是我的。谢谢！
   ① 张　　电话卡
   ② 把　　伞

5. A：这是不是你的？
   B：不是，是他的。
   ① 那　　② 那个

Assignment I

Please translate the following sentences into Chinese and read them aloud.

1. This is my watch.
2. This is Mr. Zhang's pencil.
3. Is this your cell phone?
4. Is this umbrella Jeff's?
5. That Chinese book is also John's.
6. Is that dictionary also yours?
7. That is not your letter.
8. That is not my cell phone.

Assignment II

Please use your own background to complete the following dialogues.

1. A：这是你的书吗？

   B：是的。

   A：那________是你的书吗？

   B：________________________________。

2. A：这是谁的信？

   B：________________________________。

3. A：那是不是你的衣服？

   B：______，________________________。

4. A：________________________________？

   B：不是，这是江先生的手机。

5. A：这本英文书是不是你的？

   B：________________________________。

Dì sān kè

第三课

Bàngōngshì zài èrlóu

办公室 在 二楼

Language Points

a. 办公室在二楼。
b. 林达小姐在银行。
c. 电脑不在会议室里。
d. 卡森太太在不在家？

Text

Zhèli shì shìwùsuǒ, yī lóu shì wènxùnchù hé huìkèshì.

王小姐：这里 是 事务所，一楼 是 问讯处 和 会客室。

Bàngōngshì yě zài yīlóu ma?

史密斯：办公室 也 在 一楼 吗？

Bù, bàngōngshì bù zài yīlóu, zài èrlóu.

王小姐：不，办公室 不 在 一楼，在 二楼。

Nǐ de bàngōngshì zài nǎli?

史密斯：你 的 办公室 在 哪里？

Wǒ de bàngōngshì zài èrlóu, diàntī de zuǒmiàn.

王小姐：我 的 办公室 在 二楼，电梯 的 左面。

Huìyìshì zài jǐ lóu?

史密斯：会议室 在 几 楼？

Huìyìshì yě zài èrlóu, diàntī de duìmiàn.

王小姐：会议室 也 在 二楼，电梯 的 对面。

Zhīdào le.

史密斯：知道 了。

Words

1. 办公室	bàngōngshì	(n.)	office
2. 在	zài	(v.)	be in (on, at ...)
3. 银行	yínháng	(n.)	bank
4. 电脑	diànnǎo	(n.)	computer
5. 里	lǐ	(n.)	inside
6. 太太	tàitai	(n.)	wife
7. 家	jiā	(n.)	house
8. 这里/这儿	zhèli/zhèr	(pron.)	here
9. 事务所	shìwùsuǒ	(n.)	office

10. 问讯处	wènxùnchù	(n.)	inquiry office
11. 和	hé	(conj.)	and
12. 会客室	huìkèshì	(n.)	reception room
13. 哪里/哪儿	nǎli/nǎr	(pron.)	where
14. 电梯	diàntī	(n.)	elevator
15. 左面	zuǒmiàn	(n.)	left side
16. 会议室	huìyìshì	(n.)	meeting room, assembly room
17. 几	jǐ	(pron.)	several, which
18. 对面	duìmiàn	(n.)	opposite
19. 知道	zhīdào	(v.)	know
20. 了	le	(aux.)	(expressing completion of an action)
21. 那里/那儿	nàli/nàr	(pron.)	there

Proper nouns

卡森　Kǎsēn

Supplementary words

1. 咖啡馆	kāfēiguǎn	(n.)	café
2. 书店	shūdiàn	(n.)	bookstore
3. 便利店	biànlìdiàn	(n.)	convenience store (CVS)
4. 水果店	shuíguǒdiàn	(n.)	fruit store
5. 旁边	pángbiān	(n.)	side
6. 邮局	yóujú	(n.)	post office
7. 右面	yòumiàn	(n.)	right side
8. 饭店	fàndiàn	(n.)	restaurant
9. 图书馆	túshūguǎn	(n.)	library
10. 朋友	péngyou	(n.)	friend
11. 面包店	miànbāodiàn	(n.)	bakery
12. 附近	fùjìn	(n.)	neighborhood
13. 学校	xuéxiào	(n.)	school
14. 对	duì	(adj.)	correct, right

Grammatical explanation

一、The Chinese word“在”indicating places

In expressing the meaning “in a place”, the following word order is adopted in Chinese:

person, animal or thing ＋ 在 ＋ place

For example:

(1)你的电脑在事务所。 (Your computer is in the office.)

(2)王小姐在办公室。 (Miss Wang is in the office.)

In addition to the structure “…吗?”, its question form can also be the pattern of “…是不是…?”. For example:

(1)你的电脑在不在事务所? (Is your computer in the office?)

(2)王小姐在不在办公室? (Is Miss Wang in the office?)

二、The Chinese word “不” for negation

A sentence of negation can be made by adding “不” before “是” or other verbs. For example:

(1)她不是我太太。 (She is not my wife.)

(2)他们不在学校。 (They are not in the school.)

三、“和”

The Chinese character “和” is used when more than one person or thing of the same type are enumerated. For example:

(1)我和你 (You and I)

(2)一楼、二楼和三楼 (the first floor, the second floor and the third floor)

四、“了”

The Chinese character “了” can be added to the end of a sentence to indicate “completion of an action” or “realization of something”. This is a bit different from the past tense in English. Strictly speaking, there is no so-called “past tense” in Chinese grammar. This problem will be further discussed in Chapter Seven.

Exercise I

Please read aloud the following sentences.

1. ① 这里是事务所，一楼是问讯处和会议室。
   ② 那儿是邮局，旁边是便利店和咖啡馆。
   ③ 那儿是学校，对面是书店。

2. ① 我的办公室在二楼。
   ② 我的房间在五楼。
   ③ 卡森太太的家在八楼。

3. 例：办公室在一楼吗？→ 不，办公室不在一楼。
   ① 问讯处在二楼吗？
   ② 会客室在三楼吗？
   ③ 事务所在那里吗？
   ④ 会议室在电梯的左面吗？
   ⑤ 王小姐的办公室在电梯的对面吗？

4. 例：会议室在二楼电梯的对面吗？→ 对，会议室在二楼电梯的对面。
   ① 书店在学校的对面吗？
   ② 银行在事务所的附近吗？
   ③ 邮局在便利店的左面吗？
   ④ 水果店在面包店的右面吗？
   ⑤ 饭店在咖啡馆的旁边吗？

5. 例：办公室也在二楼电梯的对面吗？→ 不对，办公室不在二楼电梯的对面。
   ① 饭店也在学校的对面吗？
   ② 水果店也在事务所的附近吗？
   ③ 银行也在便利店的左面吗？
   ④ 邮局也在面包店的右面吗？
   ⑤ 书店也在咖啡馆的旁边吗？

6. 例：他在会议室吗？→ 对，他在会议室。
   ① 林达小姐在银行吗？

② 卡森太太在咖啡馆吗?
③ 王丽丽在书店吗?
④ 江先生在办公室吗?
⑤ 她在事务所吗?

7. 例:她也在会议室吗? → 不,她不在会议室。
① 卡森太太也在银行吗?
② 王丽丽也在咖啡馆吗?
③ 林达小姐也在书店吗?
④ 他也在办公室吗?
⑤ 江先生也在事务所吗?

8. 例:她在不在会议室? → 在,她在会议室。
她在不在会议室? → 不在,她不在会议室。
① 卡森太太在不在银行?
② 王丽丽在不在咖啡馆?
③ 林达小姐在不在书店?
④ 他在不在办公室?
⑤ 江先生在不在事务所?

Exercise II

Please practice reading the following dialogues.

1. A:请问,邮局在哪儿?
B:在便利店的左面。
A:谢谢!
① 面包店　　② 水果店

2. A:林达小姐在哪儿呢?
B:她在银行。
① 书店　　② 图书馆

3. A:电脑在哪儿?
B:在办公室里。

① 手机　　房间
② 杯子　　会议室

4. A：卡森太太在不在家呢？
B：不在，她在咖啡馆。
① 朋友家　　② 便利店

5. A：你的伞在不在这儿？
B：在这儿。
① 本子　　② 铅笔

Assignment I

Please translate the following sentences into Chinese and read them aloud.

1. Where is the library?
2. The office is in Shanghai.
3. Is the convenience store near the post office?
4. Both the dictionary and the notebook are in the office.
5. Where is the IC card?
6. Mr. Carsen is in China.
7. Is Mr. Smith also in the meeting room?
8. My clothes are also in the room.

Assignment II

Please use your own background to complete the following dialogues.

1. A：你家在哪儿？
B：我家在________________。

2. A：你公司在哪儿？
B：我公司在________________。

3. A：史密斯先生在你那儿吗？

B：________________________________。

4. A：王小姐在不在事务所？

B：__________，____________________。

5. A：________________________________？

B：我的电脑在房间里。

Dì sì kè
第四课

Huìkèshì li yǒu kèrén
会客室 里 有 客人

Language Points

a. 会客室里有客人。
b. 桌子上没有电脑。
c. 他有汉语课本。
d. 她有没有中国朋友？

Text

Xiǎojie, huìkèshì li yǒu rén ma?
史密斯： 小姐，会客室 里 有 人 吗？

Yǒu rén. Shì Jiāng xiānsheng hé zǒnggōngsī de sāngè kèrén.
问讯处： 有 人。是 江 先生 和 总公司 的 三个 客人。

Nà lóushang de huìyìshì yǒuméiyǒu rén?
史密斯： 那 楼上 的 会议室 有没有 人？

Huìyìshì ma? Qǐng nín shāo děng yīxià……
问讯处： 会议室 吗？ 请 您 稍 等 一下……
Shǐmìsī xiānsheng, huìyìshì li méiyǒu rén.
史密斯 先生， 会议室 里 没有 人。

Shì ma? Xièxie!
史密斯： 是 吗？ 谢谢！

Words

1. 有	yǒu	（v.）	there is/are
2. 桌子	zhuōzi	（n.）	desk
3. 上	shàng	（n.）	upside，top
4. 课本	kèběn	（n.）	textbook
5. 没有	méiyǒu	（v.）	negation of“有”
6. 总公司	zǒnggōngsī	（n.）	parent company，head office
7. 客人	kèrén	（n.）	guest
8. 个	gè	（cl.）	（of person and thing）
9. 那	nà	（conj.）	then
10. 楼上	lóushang	（n.）	upstairs
11. 稍	shāo	（adv.）	a little
12. 等	děng	（v.）	wait
13. 一下	yīxià		a short while

Proper nouns

华盛顿 Huáshèngdùn

Supplementary words

1. 顾客	gùkè	(n.)	customer
2. 医院	yīyuàn	(n.)	hospital
3. 医生	yīshēng	(n.)	doctor
4. 病人	bìngrén	(n.)	patient
5. 教室	jiàoshì	(n.)	classroom
6. 沙发	shāfā	(n.)	sofa
7. 书架	shūjià	(n.)	bookshelf
8. 杯子	bēizi	(n.)	cup
9. 报纸	bàozhǐ	(n.)	newspaper
10. 女	nǚ	(adj.)	female
11. 哥哥	gēge	(n.)	elder brother
12. 姐姐	jiějie	(n.)	elder sister
13. 男	nán	(adj.)	male
14. 茶	chá	(n.)	tea
15. 感冒	gǎnmào	(n.,v.)	flu, to catch cold
16. 药	yào	(n.)	medicine
17. 口	kǒu	(cl.)	mouth
18. 现在	xiànzài	(n.)	present
19. 空儿	kòngr	(n.)	leisure, free time

Grammatical explanation

一、"有" indicating existence or possession

① Existence

The Chinese character "有" can be used to express "there be ... in a certain place", and the word order is as follows:

place + 有 + people (things)

It should be distinguished from "在", which expresses "... in a certain place". The word order should be:

people (things) + 在 + place

For example:

(1)教室里有学生。 (There are students in the classroom.)
(2)王先生在教室里。 (Mr. Wang is in the classroom.)
(3)书架上有报纸。 (There is newspaper on the bookshelf.)
(4)报纸在书架上。 (The newspaper is on the bookshelf.)

② Possession

In addition, the Chinese character "有" can also be used to express possession. For example:

(1)哥哥有沙发。 (My elder brother has a sofa.)
(2)姐姐有课本。 (My elder sister has a textbook.)

二、"没有" as the negative form of "有"

The negative form of "有" is not "不有", but "没有". For example:

(1)教室里没有人。 (There is nobody in the classroom.)
(2)哥哥没有沙发。 (My elder brother does not have sofa.)

三、"有没有" as a question form

Since the negation form of "有" is "没有", its question form is similar to "…是不是…?" and "…在不在…?", that is,

…有没有…?

For example:

(1)教室里有没有学生?(Are there any students in the classroom?)
(2)哥哥有没有沙发? (Does your elder brother have a sofa?)

四、Classifier for counting things

The Chinese expression "三个客人" means "three guests". In the Chinese language, when quantifiers are used, the word order should be as follows:

number + classifier + noun

For example:

(1)三张桌子 (three tables)
(2)医院里有三个医生。(There are three doctors in the hospital.)

(3)我家有四口人。 (There are four members in my family.)

五、"请…"

This Chinese character is put in the beginning of a sentence to express "Please ..." For example：

(1) 请等一下。 (Please wait a moment.)

(2) 请坐一下。 (Please sit for a while.)

六、"…一下"

The structure "verb + 一下" can be used to indicate that the action lasts "for a little while".

(1)等一下。 (Wait a moment.)

(2)请在会客室等一下。(Please wait for a little while in the reception room.)

Exercise I

Please read aloud the following sentences.

1. 例：房间里有人吗？→ 有，房间里有人。
   ① 会客室里有客人吗？
   ② 问讯处里有小姐吗？
   ③ 便利店里有店员和顾客吗？
   ④ 医院里有医生和病人吗？
   ⑤ 教室里有老师和学生吗？

2. 例：桌子上有电脑吗？→ 有，桌子上有电脑。
   ① 会客室里有沙发吗？
   ② 问讯处里有电话吗？
   ③ 书架上有书和词典吗？
   ④ 桌子上有杯子吗？
   ⑤ 沙发上有报纸吗？

3. 例：房间里有没有人？→ 有，房间里有人。
   房间里有没有人？→ 没有，房间里没有人。
   ① 会客室里有没有客人？

② 问讯处里有没有小姐？
③ 便利店里有没有店员和顾客？
④ 医院里有没有医生和病人？
⑤ 教室里有没有老师和学生？

4. 例：桌子上有没有电脑？→ 有，桌子上有电脑。
　　桌子上有没有电脑？→ 没有，桌子上没有电脑。
① 会客室里有没有沙发？
② 问讯处里有没有电话？
③ 书架上有没有书和词典？
④ 桌子上有没有杯子？
⑤ 沙发上有没有报纸？

5. 例：他有铅笔吗？→ 有，他有铅笔。
① 你有电脑吗？
② 她有手表吗？
③ 卡森太太有汉语课本吗？
④ 江先生有手机吗？
⑤ 王小姐有电话卡吗？

6. 例：他有女朋友吗？→ 有，他有女朋友。
① 你有哥哥吗？
② 她有姐姐吗？
③ 王小姐有男朋友吗？
④ 史密斯先生有太太吗？
⑤ 卡森太太有中国朋友吗？

Exercise II

Please practice reading the following dialogues.

1. A：小姐，会客室里有谁？
   B：有客人。
   ① 教室　　学生
   ② 房间　　总公司的客人

2. A：桌子上有什么？
   B：有杯子。
   ① 书架　　书和词典
   ② 沙发　　手机

3. A：史密斯先生有没有太太？
   B：有，在华盛顿。
   ① 她　　　男朋友
   ② 江先生　美国朋友

4. A：你有没有铅笔？
   B：没有。
   ① 茶　　② 感冒药

5. A：你家有几口人？
   B：五口人。
   ① 史密斯先生　四
   ② 王小姐　　　三

6. A：现在，你有空儿吗？
   B：有。
   ① 没有　　② 有

Assignment I

Please translate the following sentences into Chinese and read them aloud.

1. What are there on the sofa?
2. Are there telephone and computer in the office?
3. Is there any guest in the café?
4. Are there books and dictionaries on the bookshelves?
5. I have English textbooks.
6. I have an elder sister.
7. Mr. Smith has some Chinese friends.
8. Are you free now?

Assignment II

Please use your own background to complete the following dialogues.

1. A：你的房间里有什么？

   B：______________________________。

2. A：你的办公室里有电脑吗？

   B：______________________________。

3. A：你有姐姐吗？

   B：______________________________。

4. A：你有没有中国朋友？

   B：______________________________。

5. A：你家有几口人？

   B：______________________________。

Dì wǔ kè

第五课

Xiūxi tiān

休息天

Language Points

a. 现在十点一刻。
b. 我七点半起床。
c. 我早上七点半起床。

Text

Shǐmìsī xiānsheng, míngtiān xīngqīliù le, nín zěnme
秘　书：史密斯　先生，　明天　星期六　了，　您怎么
guò xiūxi tiān?
过　休息　天？

Nǐ shuō shénme? Wǒ bù míngbai.
史密斯：你　说　什么？　我　不　明白。

Xīngqīliù hé xīngqītiān, nín gàn shénme?
秘　书：星期六　和　星期天，　您　干　什么？

Ò, xīngqīliù wǒ dǎ gāoěrfū. Xīngqītiān shàngwǔ
史密斯：哦，　星期六　我　打　高尔夫。　星期天　上午
xǐ yīfu, xiàwǔ yī diǎn xuéxí Hànyǔ. Nǐ ne?
洗　衣服，　下午　一点　学习　汉语。　你　呢？

Wǒ xīngqīliù zài jiā, xīngqītiān kàn diànyǐng.
秘　书：我　星期六　在　家，　星期天　看　电影。

Words

1.	点	diǎn	(cl.)	o'clock
2.	刻	kè	(cl.)	fifteen minutes
3.	早上	zǎoshang	(n.)	morning
4.	半	bàn	(num.)	half, thirty minutes
5.	起床	qǐchuáng	(v.)	get up
6.	休息	xiūxi	(v.)	rest
7.	天	tiān	(n.)	day
8.	明天	míngtiān	(n.)	tomorrow
9.	星期	xīngqī	(n.)	week
10.	怎么	zěnme	(pron.)	how
11.	过	guò	(v.)	spend
12.	说	shuō	(v.)	speak, say
13.	明白	míngbai	(v.)	understand
14.	星期日/ 星期天	xīngqīrì/ xīngqītiān	(n.)	Sunday

15. 干	gàn	(v.)	do
16. 哦	ò	(int.)	ah, oh
17. 打	dǎ	(v.)	play
18. 高尔夫	gāoěrfū	(n.)	golf
19. 上午	shàngwǔ	(n.)	morning
20. 洗	xǐ	(v.)	wash
21. 下午	xiàwǔ	(n.)	afternoon
22. 学习	xuéxí	(v.)	learn, study
23. 看	kàn	(v.)	watch
24. 电影	diànyǐng	(n.)	movie, film
25. 呢	ne	(aux.)	(mark of question)

Supplementary words

1. 吧	ba	(aux.)	(indicating suggestion, request, order, etc.)
2. 晚上	wǎnshang	(n.)	evening
3. 睡觉	shuìjiào	(v.)	sleep
4. 上班	shàngbān	(v.)	work
5. 打扫	dǎsǎo	(v.)	clean, sweep
6. 见	jiàn	(v.)	see, meet
7. 左右	zuǒyòu	(aux.)	or so, about
8. 经常	jīngcháng	(adj.)	frequent
9. 听	tīng	(v.)	listen
10. 磁带	cídài	(n.)	cassette tape
11. 读	dú	(v.)	read
12. 课文	kèwén	(n.)	text
13. 差	chà	(v.)	fall short of
14. 分	fēn	(num.)	minute

Grammatical explanation

一、Subject + verb + object

The structure "subject + verb" is used in Chinese to express action. For example:

(1)我看。　　(I look.)

(2)你学习。　　(You study.)

This structure is the same as that in English, with the object after the transitive verb. For example:

(1)我看电视。　　(I watch TV.)

(2)你学习汉语。　　(You learn Chinese.)

The negation and question forms are the same as those of "是" and "在". For example:

(1)我不看电视。　　(I don't watch TV.)

(2)你学习汉语吗?　　(Do you learn Chinese?)

(3)你学习不学习汉语?　　(Do you learn Chinese?)

二、Ways of expressing time

① Time

As is in English, there are generally two ways to express the same time indicated on a clock in Chinese. For example:

(1)三点五分　　(three five)

三点过五分　　(five past three)

(2)四点三十五分　　(four thirty-five)

五点差二十五分　　(twenty-five to five)

(3)八点三十分　　(eight thirty)

八点半　　(half past eight)

There is a distinction between point of time and duration of time, which are expressed respectively by the Chinese characters "点" and "小时". For example:

(1)九点三十分　　(nine thirty)

(2)九小时三十分　　(nine hours and thirty minutes)

In the case of two o'clock, "两点" is used instead of "二点". For example:

(1)两点半(half past two)

(2)两点差五分(five to two)

(3)两点过八分(eight past two)

In the case of integral number of time duration, the quantifier "个" can be inserted between the number and "小时". For example:

(1)九个小时 (nine hours)
(2)三个半小时 (three hours and thirty minutes)

There are still some special ways to express time, as in the structures "差…分…点", "…点过…分", etc. For example:

差五分四点 (five to four) 差三分两点 (three before two)
一点过十分 (ten past one) 七点过三分 (three after seven)
两点零五分 (two five/five past two)

②Week

In expressing each day in a week, Chinese is similar to English. But there are two different ways to refer to the same day with the exception of Sunday. For example:

星期天/星期日/周日	(Sunday)
星期一/周一	(Monday)
星期二/周二	(Tuesday)
星期三/周三	(Wednesday)
星期四/周四	(Thursday)
星期五/周五	(Friday)
星期六/周六	(Saturday)

③Word order

In expressing time, Chinese differs from English in word order. In Chinese, words expressing time are normally put before the predicate verb or the subject. For example:

(1)我五点看电视。 (I watch TV at five o'clock.)
(2)你明天干什么? (What will you do tomorrow?)
(3)星期一我打扫办公室。(I clean the office on Mondays.)

三、Interrogative words "什么" and "怎么"

In the Chinese language there are 12 interrogative words which are frequently used. Among them, “什么” is concerned with “what” and “怎么” with “how”. For example:

(1)这是什么？ (What’s this?)

(2)你看什么？ (What are you looking at?)

(3)你怎么过星期天？

(How will you spend the time on Sunday? /What will you do on Sunday?)

四、Nouns + “呢”

The auxiliary word “呢” in Chinese has several meanings. Here it is used after a pronoun or noun to indicate a question, which is similar to “What about ...?” in English. For example:

(1)我学习汉语，你呢？ (I learn Chinese. And you?)

(2)这是她的，那个呢？ (This is hers. What about that?)

(3)星期天我们打高尔夫，江先生呢？

(On Sunday we’ll play golf. What about Mr. Jiang?)

Exercise I

Please read aloud the following sentences.

1. ①

差五分两点

②

六点

③

七点十五分

④

十点过五分

⑤

十二点

2. ① 他喝咖啡，你呢？

② 我去北京，你呢？

③ 我们看电影，你呢？

④ 我一点半学汉语，你呢？

⑤ 我晚上十点睡觉，你呢？

3. 例：现在七点半了吗？→ 对，七点半了。
① 现在八点一刻了吗？
② 现在九点零五分了吗？
③ 现在十点三刻了吗？
④ 现在差五分十一点了吗？
⑤ 现在十二点过五分了吗？

4. 例：你早上七点半起床吗？→ 对，我早上七点半起床。
① 她早上六点三刻起床吗？
② 张小姐晚上十一点睡觉吗？
③ 史密斯先生九点在事务所吗？
④ 王小姐八点半上班吗？
⑤ 卡森太太上午九点打扫房间吗？

5. 例：你早上七点半起床吗？→ 不，我早上七点半不起床。
① 她早上六点三刻起床吗？
② 张小姐晚上十一点睡觉吗？
③ 史密斯先生九点在事务所吗？
④ 王小姐八点半上班吗？
⑤ 卡森太太上午九点打扫房间吗？

6. 例：史密斯先生下午一点学习汉语吗？→ 对，史密斯先生下午一点学习汉语。
① 王小姐每天早上八点半在事务所吗？
② 史密斯先生十点在会议室吗？
③ 张小姐十二点不在办公室吗？
④ 江先生一点半见客人吗？
⑤ 卡森太太上午九点打扫房间吗？

Exercise II

Please practice reading the following dialogues.

1. A：请问，现在几点？
   B：五点十分。
   ① 九点过五分　　② 十一点一刻

2. A：她早上几点起床？
   B：六点半。
   ① 六点三刻　　② 七点左右

3. A：史密斯先生，您怎么过休息天？
   B：星期六打高尔夫，星期天学习汉语。
   ① 见朋友　　洗衣服
   ② 在家　　看电影

4. A：你怎么学习汉语？
   B：我经常听磁带，读课文。
   ① 英语　　② 日语

5. A：史密斯先生星期几学习汉语？
   B：星期天。
   ① 打高尔夫　　星期六
   ② 洗衣服　　星期天

Assignment I

Please translate the following sentences into Chinese and read them aloud.

1. Mr. Smith, do you also work on Saturday and Sunday?
2. Mr. Smith, what time do you learn Chinese on Sunday?
3. I'll not be in the office on Saturday and Sunday.
4. Does Mr. Wang work on Saturday and Sunday.
5. Mr. Wang stays at home on Saturday and watch movie on Sunday.
6. He always listens to tapes and read books.
7. Mrs. Carsen cleans rooms at nine in the morning.
8. Do you learn Chinese?

Assignment II

Please use your own background to complete the following dialogues.

1. A：你几点起床？几点睡觉？

   B：______________________________。

2. A：你几点上班？

   B：______________________________。

3. A：你休息天经常看电影吗？

   B：______________________________。

4. A：你怎么过星期六和星期天？

   B：______________________________。

5. A：你怎么学习汉语？

   B：______________________________。

Dì liù kè

第六课

Qù chāoshì

去 超市

Language Points

a. 我去超市。

b. 我去超市买东西。

c. 星期天,我和朋友去外滩,你去不去?

Text

(On the road)

Shǐmìsī xiānsheng!
小　周：史密斯　先生！

Xiǎo Zhōu!
史密斯：小　周！

Nǐ qù nǎr?
小　周：你　去　哪儿？

Wǒ qù chāoshì mǎi yīdiǎnr dōngxi.
史密斯：我　去　超市　买　一点儿　东西。

Shì ma? Wǒ yě qù chāoshì.
小　周：是　吗？我　也　去　超市。

Nǐ mǎi shénme?
史密斯：你　买　什么？

Wǒ mǎi diànchí. Nǐ ne?
小　周：我　买　电池。你　呢？

Wǒ mǎi diǎnr shuǐguǒ.
史密斯：我　买　点儿　水果。

(Entering the supermarket)

Diànchí shāngpǐn zài nàbiān, nǐ qùbuqù?
小　周：电池　商品　在　那边，你　去不去？

Hǎo wa. Wǒ yě qù, shùnbiàn mǎi cídài.
史密斯：好　哇。我　也　去，顺便　买　磁带。

Words

1. 去	qù	(v.)	go
2. 超市	chāoshì	(n.)	supermarket
3. 买	mǎi	(v.)	buy
4. 东西	dōngxi	(n.)	thing

5.	一点儿	yīdiǎnr	(n.)	a little
6.	电池	diànchí	(n.)	battery, cell
7.	商品	shāngpǐn	(n.)	commodity
8.	哇	wa	(aux.)	(variant of "啊")
9.	顺便	shùnbiàn	(adv.)	in passing

Proper nouns

外滩 Wàitān

Supplementary words

1.	地方	dìfang	(n.)	place
2.	喝	hē	(v.)	drink
3.	学	xué	(v.)	learn
4.	毛衣	máoyī	(n.)	sweater
5.	今晚	jīnwǎn	(n.)	tonight
6.	电视	diànshì	(n.)	television
7.	斤	jīn	(cl.)	*jin* (500 gram)
8.	寄	jì	(v.)	send, post, mail
9.	封	fēng	(cl.)	(of letter)
10.	地铁站	dìtiězhàn	(n.)	subway station
11.	美容院	měiróngyuàn	(n.)	beauty parlor, beauty salon
12.	包	bāo	(cl.)	package
13.	饼干	bǐnggān	(n.)	biscuit, cookies
14.	条	tiáo	(cl.)	(of thin and long things)
15.	毛巾	máojīn	(n.)	towel
16.	逛	guàng	(v.)	ramble
17.	街	jiē	(n.)	street
18.	对不起	duìbuqǐ		sorry, excuse me
19.	牛奶	niúnǎi	(n.)	milk
20.	红茶	hóngchá	(n.)	black tea

21. 茉莉花茶	mòlìhuāchá	(n.)	jasmine tea
22. 步行街	bùxíngjiē	(n.)	pedestrian street

Grammatical explanation

一、"去" + place

To express "go to a place", the Chinese structure "去 + place" is used. For example:

(1)小周去医院。 (Mr. Zhou will go to the hospital.)
(2)你去美容院吗? (Will you go to the beauty salon?)
(3)我去教室。 (I'm going to the classroom.)
(4)她们不去会客室。 (They will not go to the reception room.)

二、To go to a place to do something

In Chinese actions are organized according to the time sequence. The order for "to go to a place to do something" is as follows:

去 + place + action

For example:

(1)我去超市买磁带。 (I'll go to the supermarket to buy tapes.)
(2)你去便利店买什么? (What will you go to the convenience store to buy?)
(3)王小姐去房间看电视。(Miss Wang will go to her room to watch TV.)

三、"和"

The character "和" has been introduced in Lesson Three. It means "and" and is used to enumerate things of the same kind, such as "我和你"(You and I) and "邮局和银行"(post office and bank).

It is a little different in this lesson and means "to do something with", as in the structure "…和…一起,做…". For example:

(1)管理员和史密斯先生去会议室。
(The administrator and Mr. Smith will go to the meeting room.)
(2)你和谁去打高尔夫? (Who will you go to play golf with?)

四、“哇”

In Chinese there are many characters which are used at the end of sentences to indicate the personal feeling of the speaker, such as “啊”, “呢”, etc. There is no such word in the English language. Due to the influence of the sound before it, the character “啊” may be prounced with some changes. The character “哇” is one of its variations. For example:

“你有没有手机?”“有哇。”

(“Do you have a cell phone?” “Yes, I have.”)

Exercise I

Please read aloud the following sentences.

1. ① 你去哪儿?
   ② 史密斯先生去哪儿?
   ③ 小周去什么地方?

2. ① 我去超市买一点儿东西。
   ② 史密斯先生去超市买水果。
   ③ 小周去超市买电池。
   ④ 卡森太太去咖啡馆喝咖啡。
   ⑤ 小张去学校学英语。

3. ① 电池商品在那边,你去不去?
   ② 明天我去步行街,你去不去?
   ③ 这是茉莉花茶,你喝不喝?
   ④ 这件毛衣你买不买?
   ⑤ 今晚的电视你看不看?

4. ① 我买电池。
   ② 我听磁带。
   ③ 他买一本书。
   ④ 江先生寄一封信。
   ⑤ 我买一点儿水果。

5. 例：史密斯先生去买水果吗？→ 对，史密斯先生去买水果。
   ① 小周去超市买电池吗？
   ② 卡森太太去咖啡馆喝咖啡吗？
   ③ 小张去学校学英语吗？
   ④ 王小姐去书店买书吗？
   ⑤ 江先生去邮局寄信吗？

6. 例：史密斯先生去买电池吗？→ 不，史密斯先生不去买电池。
   ① 小周去超市买电池吗？
   ② 江先生去咖啡馆喝咖啡吗？
   ③ 卡森太太去学校学英语吗？
   ④ 张小姐去书店买书吗？
   ⑤ 王小姐去邮局寄信吗？

Exercise II

Please practice reading the following dialogues.

1. A：你去哪儿？
   B：我去超市。
   ① 地铁站　　② 美容院

2. A：你去超市买什么？
   B：我买电池。
   ① 饼干　　② 毛巾

3. A：星期天我和朋友去外滩，你去不去？
   B：好哇。
   ① 逛街　　② 看电影

4. A：小张，你喝不喝茶？
   B：对不起，我不喝。
   ① 牛奶　　② 红茶

Assignment I

Please translate the following sentences into Chinese and read them aloud.

1. Where are you going?
2. I'll go to the beauty salon. And you?
3. I'll go to the pedestrian street tomorrow. What about you?
4. I often go window-shopping with friends on Sunday.
5. Mrs. Carsen will go to the supermarket to buy cookies.
6. I'll go to the department store to buy clothes.
7. She will go to the convenience store to buy black tea.
8. On Sunday Mr. Smith will go to play golf with his friends.

Assignment II

Please use your own background to complete the following dialogues.

1. A：你去哪儿？

   B：____________________________。

2. A：休息天，你经常去哪儿？干什么？

   B：____________________________。

3. A：我和王小姐去咖啡馆喝茶，你去不去？

   B：____________________________。

4. A：这是中国红茶，你喝不喝？

   B：____________________________。

5. A：你经常看中国电视吗？

   B：____________________________。

Dì qī kè
第七课

Jiàn péngyou
见 朋友

Language Points

a. 他在书店买杂志。
b. 李小姐(正)在打电话。
c. 我们买一点儿礼物,怎么样?

Text

(The apartment doorman is calling Mr. Smith.)

Wèi, nín shì sìshíbāshì de Shǐmìsī xiānsheng ma?
公寓门卫：喂，您是48室的史密斯先生吗？

Shì a, nǐ shì……
史密斯：是啊，你是……

Wǒ shì ménwèi. Lóuxià yǒu rén zhǎo nín.
公寓门卫：我是门卫。楼下有人找您。

Xièxie. Wǒ mǎshàng xiàqu.
史密斯：谢谢。我马上下去。

(In the lobby of the apartment)

Shǐmìsī xiānsheng, hǎojiǔ bù jiàn le!
布朗夫妇：史密斯先生，好久不见了！

Hǎojiǔ bù jiàn le! Wǒ zhèngzài děng nǐmen ne.
史密斯：好久不见了！我正在等你们呢。

Shì ma? Wǒmen xiān qù bīnguǎn, zài nàr jì xíngli le.
布朗：是吗？我们先去宾馆，在那儿寄行李了。

Bùlǎng fūrén dì yī cì lái Zhōngguó, shì ma?
史密斯：布朗夫人第一次来中国，是吗？

Shì.
布朗夫人：是。

Míngtiān wǒ xiūxi, dài nǐmen qù Pǔdōng wánr, zěnmeyàng?
史密斯：明天我休息，带你们去浦东玩儿，怎么样？

Xièxie!
布朗夫妇：谢谢！

Words

1. 在	zài	(prep.)	in, at
2. 杂志	zázhì	(n.)	magazine
3. 正在	zhèngzài	(adv.)	(indicating the continuation of action)
4. 电话	diànhuà	(n.)	telephone
5. 礼物	lǐwù	(n.)	gift
6. 怎么样	zěnmeyàng	(pron.)	how about
7. 门卫	ménwèi	(n.)	doorman
8. 找	zhǎo	(v.)	look for
9. 马上	mǎshàng	(adv.)	at once
10. 下去	xiàqu		go downstairs
11. 好久	hǎojiǔ	(n.)	a long time
12. 了	le	(aux.)	(indicating the completion of an action)
13. 呢	ne	(aux.)	(indicating affirmation)
14. 先	xiān	(adv.)	first
15. 宾馆	bīnguǎn	(n.)	guesthouse
16. 寄	jì	(v.)	send, mail
17. 行李	xíngli	(n.)	luggage
18. 第	dì	(prefix.)	(used before numbers to indicate order)
19. 次	cì	(cl.)	times
20. 带	dài	(v.)	bring, take
21. 玩儿	wánr	(v.)	play
22. 喂	wèi	(int.)	hello
23. 啊	a	(aux.)	(expressing surprise, promise, etc)

Proper nouns

(一)		(二)	
罗斯	Luósī	浦东	Pǔdong

Supplementary words

1. 来	lái	(v.)	come
2. 菜	cài	(n.)	dish
3. 旅游	lǚyóu	(v.)	tour
4. 做	zuò	(v.)	do
5. 饭	fàn	(n.)	meal

Grammatical explanation

一、"了" as the auxiliary word of mood at the end of sentence

The word "了" is used to express changes of situations, occurrence of new situations or recognition of a certain change. For example:

(1) 我的书没有了。 (My book has disappeared.)

(2) 她不来了。 (She won't come.)

二、"了" indicating completion

① "了" can be used to indicate the completion or realization of an action. When Chinese sentences with "了" are translated into English, the tense can be past, perfect past or future, which depends on the concrete situation of context. Therefore, "了" does not mean past tense in Chinese and it is believed that there is no past tense in Chinese language. Whether this word should be used or not in the translation from English into Chinese relies on the context. This deserves necessary attention. For example:

(1)我买了。 (I have bought some.)

(2)他打扫了。 (He swept the floor.)

(3)秘书来了。 (The secretary has come.)

② Sentence with object

Whether there is object in a sentence, and whether the object is used in isolation or with other modifiers-all this influences the use of "了".

a. Object used in isolation

寄行李了。 (Luggage has been sent.)

In the example sentence, "了" is used in the end. The sentence can be changed into "寄了行李了" without considerable change of meaning.

b. Object used with modifier

寄了两个行李。　　（Two pieces of luggage were sent.）

Here "了" is used after the verb. But the sentence can also be changed into "寄了两个行李了".

三、"在" + nouns of place + verb

This structure is used to indicate that an action happens at a certain place. For example:

(1)周先生在便利店买东西。
（Mr. Zhou is shopping in the convenience store.）

(2)你在咖啡店喝牛奶吗?
（Are you drinking milk in the café?）

四、"(正)在" + verb + object(+ 呢)

① Another important usage of "在" is to put it before verb to indicate progressive tense. For example:

(1)她们在看电影。　　（They are watching movie.）

(2)我在找我太太。　　（I'm looking for my wife.）

② A summary of "在"

a. Used as a verb

布朗先生在学校。　　（Mr. Brown is in the school.）

b. Used as a preposition

布朗先生在学校学汉语。（Mr. Brown learns Chinese at school.）

c. Used to indicate progressive tense

布朗先生在学汉语。　　（Mr. Brown is learning English.）

③ Combination of both b and c?

It is not natural to say "布朗先生在学校在学汉语", which should be changed into "布朗先生正在学校学汉语".

五、"…，怎么样？"

This structure means a suggestion, similar to "What about . . . ?" or "How about . . . ?" in English. For example：

(1)我们去看电影，怎么样？（What about going to movie? /Shall we go to movie together?）

(2)这个怎么样？（What /How about this?）

六、"是啊"

This is one way to express agreement with others. For example：

是啊，他就是我们的总经理。

（Yes, he is the very general manager of ours.）

Exercise I

Please read aloud the following sentences.

1. ① 我们先去宾馆。
② 我先买杂志。
③ 他先来上海。
④ 王小姐先打电话。
⑤ 史密斯先生先见朋友。

2. ① 我们在那儿寄行李了。
② 我在书店买杂志了。
③ 史密斯先生在上海见朋友。
④ 他在地铁站等女朋友。
⑤ 小张在办公室打电话。

3. ① 明天我休息，带你们去浦东玩儿，怎么样？
② 我们买一点儿礼物，怎么样？
③ 星期天我们去打高尔夫，怎么样？
④ 晚上我们一起吃中国菜，怎么样？
⑤ 下午，你来我的房间玩儿，怎么样？

4. 例：史密斯先生正在等布朗夫妇吗？→ 对，史密斯先生正在等布朗夫妇。

① 布朗夫妇正在寄行李吗?
② 她正在买书吗?
③ 史密斯先生正在见朋友吗?
④ 他正在等女朋友吗?
⑤ 李小姐正在打电话吗?

5. 例:史密斯夫人第一次来中国吗? → 是,她第一次来中国。
① 她第一次吃美国菜吗?
② 你第一次看中国电影吗?
③ 史密斯先生第一次来上海吗?
④ 江先生第一次去北京吗?
⑤ 王小姐的哥哥第一次去美国旅游吗?

Exercise II

Please practice reading the following dialogues.

1. A:喂,您是48 室的史密斯先生吗?
B:是啊,你是……
A:我是门卫。
① 软件公司的总经理　　江先生的朋友
② 罗斯小姐　　北京公司的小李

2. A:史密斯先生,楼下有人找你。
B:谢谢。我马上下去。
① 张小姐　　有您的电话
② 布朗先生　　有你的信

3. A:我正在等你们呢。
B:是吗?我们先去宾馆,在那儿寄行李了。
① 图书馆　　借书了
② 房间　　休息了一会儿

4. A:罗斯,你在干什么?
B:我在看书呢。

① 洗衣服　　　　② 做饭

5. A：最近你在学汉语吗？
 B：我在学汉语。
 ① 打高尔夫　　② 学电脑

Assignment I

Please translate the following sentences into Chinese and read them aloud.

1. I'm learning Chinese at school.
2. Mr. Smith is meeting his friends.
3. What about taking some coffee here?
4. How about watching movie on Sunday?
5. I went to my company to place a telephone call just now.
6. Is this the first time that you come to Shanghai?
7. I watched the Chinese movie in Beijing for the first time.
8. Where will Mr. Smith bring Mr. and Mrs. Brown to have a visit?

Assignment II

Please use your own background to complete the following dialogues.

1. A：最近，你在干什么？

 B：______________________________。

2. A：你在学汉语吗？

 B：______________________________。

3. A：休息天，你经常在哪儿买东西？

 B：______________________________。

4. A：你第一次来中国吗？

 B：______________________________。

5. A：明天我们去逛步行街，怎么样？

B：______________________________。

Dì bā kè

第八课

Qù cānguān Dōngfāng Míngzhū Diànshìtǎ

去 参观 东方 明珠 电视塔

Language Points

a. 南京路很热闹。

b. 北京的夏天热不热？

c. 浦东陆家嘴路的大厦又高又漂亮。

Text

(In a taxi)

	Sījī, qiánmian shì suìdào ma?
史密斯：	司机，前面是隧道吗？
	Duì, guò le suìdào jiù dào Pǔdōng le.
司　机：	对，过了隧道就到浦东了。
	Zhèli jiù shì Pǔdōng.
史密斯：	这里就是浦东。
	Pǔdōng de mǎlù zhēn kuān a.
布朗夫人：	浦东的马路真宽啊。
	Zhèli de dàshà yòu gāo yòu piàoliang.
布　朗：	这里的大厦又高又漂亮。
	Nǐmen kàn, nà jiù shì Dōngfāng Míngzhū Diànshìtǎ.
史密斯：	你们看，那就是东方明珠电视塔。
	Zhēn gāo wa!
布朗夫妇：	真高哇！
	Dōngfāng Míngzhū Diànshìtǎ dào le. Kèrénmen, qǐng bù yào wàngjì zìjǐ de dōngxi.
司　机：	东方明珠电视塔到了。客人们，请不要忘记自己的东西。
	Xièxie!
史密斯： 布朗夫妇：	谢谢！

Words

1. 路	lù	(n.)	road
2. 很	hěn	(adv.)	very
3. 热闹	rènao	(adj.)	hilarious
4. 夏天	xiàtiān	(n.)	summer
5. 热	rè	(adj.)	hot

6. 大厦	dàshà	(n.)	high-rise
7. 又…又…	yòu…yòu…		both ... and ...
8. 高	gāo	(adj.)	high
9. 漂亮	piàoliang	(adj.)	beautiful, wonderful
10. 参观	cānguān	(v.)	visit
11. 司机	sījī	(n.)	driver
12. 隧道	suìdào	(n.)	tunnel
13. 过	guò	(v.)	pass
14. 就	jiù	(adv.)	at once
15. 到	dào	(v.)	reach, arrive at
16. 马路	mǎlù	(n.)	street
17. 真	zhēn	(adv.)	really
18. 宽	kuān	(adj.)	wide
19. 不要	bùyào	(adv.)	don't
20. 忘记	wàngjì	(v.)	forget
21. 自己	zìjǐ	(pron.)	oneself
22. 夫人	fūrén	(n.)	Mrs., madam
23. 夫妇	fūfù	(n.)	husband and wife

Proper nouns

1. 南京	Nánjīng
2. 陆家嘴	Lùjiāzuǐ
3. 东方明珠电视塔	Dōngfāng Míngzhū Diànshìtǎ
4. 人民广场	Rénmín Guǎngchǎng
5. 杨浦大桥	Yángpǔ Dàqiáo
6. 南浦大桥	Nánpǔ Dàqiáo
7. 金茂大厦	Jīnmào Dàshà
8. 上海商城	Shànghǎi Shāngchéng

Supplementary words

1. 红绿灯	hónglǜdēng	(n.)	traffic lights
2. 便宜	piányi	(adj.)	cheap
3. 好吃	hǎochī	(adj.)	delicious
4. 干净	gānjìng	(adj.)	clean
5. 家	jiā	(cl.)	(of family, shop, company, etc.)
6. 好看	hǎokàn	(adj.)	good-looking
7. 贵	guì	(adj.)	expensive
8. 小	xiǎo	(adj.)	small
9. 脏	zāng	(adj.)	dirty

Grammatical explanation

一、Adverbs such as "很", "非常" and "真" + adjectives

Adverbs of degree such as "非常", "稍微", "最", etc. are generally used before adjectives. Three of them are introduced in this lesson. It's very easy, putting an adverb before adjectives. For example:

(1)很干净。　(Very clean.)

(2)非常好。　(Very good.)

(3)真好吃。　(Really delicious.)

♣Note:

Adjectives in Chinese language fall into two categories: those of nature and those of state. The adjectives such as "干净", "好", "好吃" ... are of nature. They are seldom used in isolation in sentences. For example, the sentence "南京路热闹" does not sound natural, since it leaves an impression of comparison like "南京路是很热闹,但…路就…". Treated in the following way, i.e. adding an adverb before the adjective, the sentence will be more natural:

南京路很热闹。 (The atmosphere is lively in Nanjing Road.)

Here "很" is merely used to make the sentence sound natural while it does not mean "very".

二、"热不热"

The basic sentence structure of question for adjectives is the pattern "…吗?". Another form of question is similar to the question form of "是" and other verbs-combination of both affirmation and negation, such as "是不是". In these two types of question form, it is not necessary to add "很" before adjectives, as is the case in the above note. For example:

(1)上海的马路宽不宽？ (Are the roads in Shanghai wide?)

(2)东方明珠电视塔高不高?(Is the Oriental Pearl TV Tower high?)

三、"又…又…"

This structure is used in enumerating actions or states. For example:

(1)我的毛衣又便宜又漂亮。(My sweater is both cheap and beautiful.)

(2)浦东的马路又宽又干净。(Roads in Pudong are both wide and clean.)

四、"你们看，…"

In Chinese, common sentence patterns can be used to express commands. The sentence "你们看" does not mean "你们大家在看"(All of you are looking), but mean "请看"(Look, please.)

五、Antonyms of common adjectives

In the following some adjectives and their antonyms will be introduced.

热闹⇔安静 ānjìng (silent)	热⇔冷 lěng (cold)
高⇔低 dī (low)	宽⇔窄 zhǎi (narrow)
便宜⇔贵	干净⇔脏
大 dà (big)⇔小	暖和 nuǎnhuo (warm)⇔ 凉快 liángkuai (cool)

六、Expressions of season

春天 chūntiān (spring)、夏天 xiàtiān (summer)、秋天 qiūtiān (autumn)、冬天 dōngtiān (winter)

Exercise I

Please read aloud the following sentences.

1. ① 过了隧道就到浦东了。
   ② 过了这条马路就到学校了。
   ③ 过了红绿灯就到便利店了。

2. ① 浦东的马路真宽啊。
   ② 上海真热闹啊。
   ③ 这里的水果真便宜啊。
   ④ 她的衣服真漂亮啊。
   ⑤ 中国菜真好吃啊。

3. ① 这里的大厦又高又漂亮。
   ② 那条马路又宽又干净。
   ③ 那家饭店的菜又好吃又便宜。
   ④ 这件衣服又不好看又贵。
   ⑤ 这个地方又小又脏。

4. ① 你们看,那就是东方明珠电视塔。
   ② 你看,这就是我的手机。
   ③ 你看,这就是我的房间。
   ④ 你们看,这儿就是我们的教室。
   ⑤ 你们看,这就是我的办公室。

5. ① 北京的夏天热不热?
   ② 南京路热闹不热闹?
   ③ 那家饭店的菜好吃不好吃?
   ④ 这里的水果贵不贵?
   ⑤ 浦东的马路宽不宽?

6. ① 北京的夏天热吗?
   ② 南京路热闹吗?
   ③ 那家饭店的菜好吃吗?
   ④ 这里的水果贵吗?

⑤ 浦东的马路宽吗？

Exercise II

Please practice reading the following dialogues.

1. A：司机，前面是隧道吗？
   B：对，过了隧道就到浦东了。
   ① 杨浦大桥　　② 南浦大桥

2. A：这里就是浦东。
   B：浦东的马路真宽啊。
   ① 外滩　　　　漂亮
   ② 人民广场　　大

3. A：北京的夏天热不热？
   B：很热。
   ① 水果　　便宜不便宜　　便宜
   ② 马路　　宽不宽　　　　宽

4. A：小张，昨天我和朋友去参观了东方明珠电视塔。
   B：是吗？
   A：东方明珠电视塔又高又漂亮。
   ① 金茂大厦　　②上海商城

Assignment I

Please translate the following sentences into Chinese and read them aloud.

1. Today the People's Square is very busy.
2. Is winter in Shanghai cold?
3. The road is both wide and clean.
4. These clothes are both beautiful and cheap.
5. The Jinmao Building is really high.
6. Are the dishes in this restaurant delicious?
7. It is both quiet and clean around the school.
8. The building of our company is both large and high.

Assignment II

Please use your own background to complete the following dialogues.

1. A：最近，你去浦东了吗？

   B：______________________________。

2. A：我家附近很安静，你家附近呢？

   B：______________________________。

3. A：纽约冬天冷不冷？ 夏天热不热？

   B：______________________________。

4. A：那家饭店又好吃又便宜，星期天我们去那里吃饭，怎么样？

   B：______________________________。

5. A：你们公司的大厦高吗？

   B：______________________________。

Dì jiǔ kè
第九课

Tā gǎnmào le
他感冒了

Language Points

a. 他病了，因此今天不上班。
b. 因为下雨，所以我不去超市了。
c. 你会说中国话吗？

Text

Shǐmìsī xiānsheng, nín zěnme le?
秘　书：史密斯　先生，　您　怎么　了？

Wǒ tóu téng, késou.
史密斯：我　头　疼，　咳嗽。

Qù yīyuàn le ma?
秘　书：去　医院　了　吗？

Qù le. Yīshēng shuō shì gǎnmào, yīncǐ gěi wǒ
史密斯：去　了。　医生　说　是　感冒，　因此　给　我
kāi le yīdiǎnr gǎnmào chōngjì.
开　了　一点儿　感冒　冲剂。

Nín huì hē gǎnmào chōngjì?
秘　书：您　会　喝　感冒　冲剂？

Duì, yīnwèi zhōngyào fùzuòyòng shǎo, suǒyǐ wǒ
史密斯：对，　因为　中药　副作用　少，　所以　我
xǐhuan chī zhōngyào.
喜欢　吃　中药。

Shì ma? Bùguò, nín chī le yào hái yào hǎohāor
秘　书：是　吗？　不过，　您　吃　了　药　还　要　好好儿
xiūxixiūxi.
休息休息。

Míngbai le.
史密斯：明白　了。

Words

1. 病	bìng	(n.)	disease
2. 因此	yīncǐ	(conj.)	since
3. 因为…	yīnwèi…		because
4. 下	xià	(v.)	fall
5. 雨	yǔ	(n.)	rain
6. 会	huì	(aux., v.)	can

7. 头	tóu	(n.)	head
8. 疼	téng	(v.)	ache
9. 咳嗽	késou	(v.)	cough
10. 给	gěi	(v., prep.)	give
11. 开	kāi	(v.)	open
12. 冲剂	chōngjì	(n.)	granules
13. 吃	chī	(n.)	eat, take
14. 中药	zhōngyào	(n.)	traditional Chinese medicine
15. 副	fù	(adj.)	vice, deputy
16. 作用	zuòyòng	(n.)	function
17. 少	shǎo	(adj.)	few, little
18. 喜欢	xǐhuan	(v.)	like
19. 不过	bùguò	(conj.)	but
20. 还	hái	(adv.)	also
21. 要	yào	(v.)	have to
22. 好好儿	hǎohāor	(adj.)	good
23. 今天	jīntiān	(n.)	today

Proper nouns

广州　Guǎngzhōu

Supplementary words

1. 巴士	bāshì	(n.)	bus
2. 忙	máng	(adj.)	busy
3. 进	jìn	(v.)	enter
4. 游泳	yóuyǒng	(v.)	swim
5. 酒	jiǔ	(n.)	wine
6. 嗓子	sǎngzi	(n.)	throat
7. 胃	wèi	(n.)	stomach
8. 回	huí	(v.)	return

9. 啤酒	píjiǔ	(n.)	beer
10. 昨天	zuótiān	(n.)	yesterday

Grammatical explanation

一、"因此"、and "因为…所以…"

To express causes or reasons, the following two structures are often used:

(由于)…,因此…

因为…,所以…

But the structure "因为…,因此…" is not acceptable in Chinese language.

(1)中药副作用少,因此我喜欢吃中药。

(Since traditional Chinese medicine has less side effects, I like it.)

(2)因为头疼,所以我去医院。

(Since I had a headache, I went to hospital.)

二、"怎么了"

The expression "怎么" has been learned in Lesson Five where it is an interrogative word with the meaning "how". With the additional auxiliary word "了" after it, the structure expresses a past action.

她不在公司,也不在学校。她怎么了?

(She is neither in the company nor at home. How is she?)

三、Repetition of verbs: "休息休息"

Repetition of verbs has the meaning of "a little" or "have a try to do". It depends on the context to decide whether the meaning of this kind of repetition is different from the original verb. However, the structure of repetition is more colloquial. Moreover, the repetition of a verb consisting of one character sometimes has "一" between the two characters and the meaning remains unchanged.

(1)我看看电视。 (I'll watch TV.)

(2)我洗洗衣服。 (I'll wash my clothes.)

(3)我听一听磁带。 (I'll listen to tapes.)

四、"要"

There are some special verbs in Chinese language which mean "desire", "permission", "possibility", etc. They are called modal verbs. The word "要" is one of them, which has three basic meanings. It is used in this lesson with the meaning of "must" and "have to".

今天很忙，我们还要去别的公司。

（Today we are very busy and we must go to visit other companies.）

♣Note：

The negation form of the word "要" here is not "不要", since the latter generally means "mustn't". The negative form of "要" in this lesson is used with the meaning of "needn't".

五、"会" with the meaning of "ability"

The word "会" is also a modal verb, which has two meanings. The word in this lesson has the meaning of "may" or "can".

（1）她会说汉语。　　（She can speak Chinese.）

（2）我会英语。　　（I know English.）

Exercise I

Please read aloud the following sentences.

1. ① 医生说是感冒，因此给我开了一点儿感冒冲剂。
   ② 他病了，因此今天不上班了。
   ③ 天冷了，因此我坐巴士去公司。
   ④ 今天我很忙，因此不去看电影了。
   ⑤ 这件衣服很贵，因此我不买了。

2. ① 因为中药副作用少，所以我喜欢吃中药。
   ② 因为下雨，所以我不去超市了。
   ③ 因为头疼咳嗽，所以我去医院了。
   ④ 因为我在中国工作，所以正在学习汉语。
   ⑤ 因为他喜欢红茶，所以经常喝红茶。

3. ① 我喜欢吃中药。

② 我喜欢看电影。
③ 他喜欢逛马路。
④ 卡森太太喜欢喝咖啡。
⑤ 史密斯先生喜欢打高尔夫。

4. ① 吃了药还要好好儿休息休息。
② 到中国还要好好儿玩儿玩儿。
③ 史密斯先生到了上海还要去北京。
④ 进了公司还要好好儿工作。
⑤ 学了英语还要学日语。

5. 例：史密斯先生感冒了？→ 是的，他感冒了。
① 你下班了？
② 她去美国了？
③ 最近，江先生买电脑了？
④ 史密斯先生去医院了？
⑤ 他病了？

6. 例：你会说中国话吗？→ 不，我不会说中国话。
① 你会游泳吗？
② 他会电脑吗？
③ 王小姐会做美国菜吗？
④ 你会喝酒吗？
⑤ 小张会说英语吗？

Exercise II

Please practice reading the following dialogues.

1. A：史密斯先生，您怎么了？
B：我头疼，咳嗽。
① 林达小姐　　嗓子疼
② 江先生　　胃疼

2. A：你去医院了吗？

B：去了。医生说是感冒了，因此给我开了一点儿感冒冲剂。
① 逛街　　下雨了，因此马上回家了。
② 北京　　天冷了，因此我昨天回广州了。

3. A：你喜欢喝什么？
B：我喜欢喝咖啡。
① 中国红茶　　② 美国啤酒

4. A：你会不会说中国话？
B：会一点儿。
① 做菜　　② 游泳

Assignment I

Please translate the following sentences into Chinese and read them aloud.

1. Because I caught a cold yesterday, I took a rest.
2. Because my stomach ached, I went to hospital.
3. Because this dictionary is very expensive, I didn't buy one.
4. Can you read books in Chinese?
5. Can she cook Chinese dishes?
6. Mr. Smith likes to drink beer.
7. Do you like travel?
8. I don't like window-shopping.

Assignment II

Please use your own background to complete the following dialogues.

1. A：你喜欢喝啤酒吗？
B：________________。

2. A：在中国，你喜欢去哪儿玩儿？
B：________________。

3. A：你会喝中药吗？

   B：________________________________。

4. A：你经常感冒吗？

   B：________________________________。

5. A：我会说一点儿中国话，你呢？

   B：________________________________。

Dì shí kè

第十课

Shēngri

生日

Language Points

a. 她的年纪跟/和/同我一样大。
b. 这里的春天这么暖和。
c. 那太好了。

Text

(After work)

Shǐmìsī xiānsheng, jīntiān shì nín lái Shànghǎi yǐhòu
小　张：史密斯　先生，今天　是　您　来　上海　以后
dìyīcì guò shēngri, duì ma?
第一次　过　生日，对　吗？

Duì, duì.
史密斯：对，对。

Zhù nín shēngri kuàilè!
同事们：祝　您　生日　快乐！

Xièxie dàjiā!
史密斯：谢谢　大家！

Shǐmìsī xiānsheng, zhè shì dàjiā sòng nín de
江先生：史密斯　先生，这　是　大家　送　您　的
shēngri dàngāo.
生日　蛋糕。

Zhème dà de dàngāo! Zài Měiguó guò shēngri de
史密斯：这么　大　的　蛋糕！在　美国　过　生日　的
shíhou, wǒ tàitai sòng wǒ dàngāo. Jīntiān dàjiā
时候，我　太太　送　我　蛋糕。今天　大家
sòng wǒ dàngāo, wǒ juéde gēn zài Měiguó yīyàng,
送　我　蛋糕，我　觉得　跟　在　美国　一样，
fēicháng gāoxìng.
非常　高兴。

Nà tài hǎo le!
江先生：那　太　好　了！

Wǒ jiànyì: xiànzài Shǐmìsī xiānsheng chuī làzhú
王小姐：我　建议：现在　史密斯　先生　吹　蜡烛
qiē dàngāo, ránhòu dàjiā chàng《Zhùnǐ shēngri kuàilè》,
切　蛋糕，然后　大家　唱《祝你　生日　快乐》，
hǎo ma?
好　吗？

Hǎo!
同事们：好！

Words

1.	以后	yǐhòu		after
2.	生日	shēngri	(n.)	birthday
3.	祝	zhù	(v.)	wish
4.	快乐	kuàilè	(adj.)	happy
5.	大家	dàjiā	(n.)	everybody
6.	送	sòng	(v.)	give present to
7.	蛋糕	dàngāo	(n.)	cake
8.	这么	zhème	(pron.)	such
9.	大	dà	(adj.)	big
10.	时候	shíhou	(n.)	when
11.	觉得	juéde	(v.)	feel
12.	跟/和/同…一样	gēn/hé/tóng…yīyàng		the same as
13.	非常	fēicháng	(adv.)	very
14.	高兴	gāoxìng	(adj.)	happy
15.	太…了	tài…le		too, very
16.	建议	jiànyì	(v.)	suggest
17.	吹	chuī	(v.)	blow
18.	蜡烛	làzhú	(n.)	candle
19.	切	qiē	(v.)	cut
20.	然后	ránhòu	(adv.)	afterwards
21.	唱	chàng	(v.)	sing
22.	年纪	niánjì	(n.)	age
23.	各	gè	(pron.)	every
24.	同事	tóngshì	(n.)	colleague

Proper nouns

1.	《祝你生日快乐》	《Zhùnǐ shēngri kuàilè》
2.	香港	Xiānggǎng

Supplementary words

1. 随便	suíbiàn	(adj.)	imformal
2. 个子	gèzi	(n.)	stature
3. 顺利	shùnlì	(adj.)	favoring
4. 进步	jìnbù	(v., adj.)	progress
5. 句	jù	(cl.)	(used of sentences)
6. 话	huà	(n.)	remark
7. 干杯	gānbēi		cheers

Grammatical explanation

一、"跟/和/同…一样"

There are three ways of comparison in Chinese language:

1. 和…一样(as ... as)
2. 比…(more than)
3. 最…(most)

The structure "和…一样" introduced in this lesson has the same meaning as "as ... as ..." or "the same as". It is a combination of "跟/和/同" and "一样"。

(1)美国蛋糕跟中国的一样。(The American cakes are the same as Chinese ones.)

(2)我的跟你的一样。(Mine is the same as yours.)

To explain in what sense two things are similar, i.e. the content of similarity, supplementary explanations are added after "一样".

(1)美国蛋糕跟中国的一样好吃。(The American cakes are as delicious as Chinese ones.)

(2)我的跟你的一样便宜。(Mine is as cheap as yours.)

二、"这么/那么…"

This structure means "so" or "such" in English.

The "这么/那么…" can be followed by adjectives.

(1)他的电脑那么贵。(His computer is so expensive.)

(2)这么漂亮的房间啊。(What a beautiful room!)

The “这么/那么…” can also be followed by verbs.

(1)啤酒的“啤”字这么写。 (The character “啤” as in “啤酒” is written like this.)

(2)大家都那么说。 (Everybody said the same thing.)

三、“太…了”

This structure has the meaning of “非常”(very). It is often used to express such a derogatory meaning as “excess”.

(1)太好了! (Very good!)

(2)太高兴了! (I'm very happy!)

(3)太贵了! (Too expensive!)

(4)太大了! (Too big!)

Exercise I

Please read aloud the following sentences.

1. ① 这是大家送您的生日蛋糕。
   ② 这是我送你的生日礼物。
   ③ 那是她做的菜。
   ④ 这是我买的衣服。
   ⑤ 那是他们干的工作。

2. ① 这么大的蛋糕!
   ② 那么漂亮的房间。
   ③ 这里的春天这么暖和。
   ④ 她是这么好的朋友。
   ⑤ 你的手机那么贵。

3. ① 我觉得跟在美国一样,非常高兴。
   ② 我觉得跟在家里一样,很随便。
   ③ 她的年纪跟我一样大。
   ④ 小张的个子跟我一样高。
   ⑤ 他的手表跟江先生的一样。

Exercise II

Please practice reading the following dialogues.

1. A：今天，是您来上海以后第一次过生日，对吗？
   B：对，对。
   ① 看中国电影　　② 逛街

2. A：祝您生日快乐！
   B：谢谢！
   ① 工作顺利　　② 学习进步

3. A：我建议：史密斯先生吹蜡烛，切蛋糕，然后大家唱《祝你生日快乐》，好吗？
   B：好！
   ① 唱美国歌　　唱中国歌
   ② 说一句话　　干杯

Assignment I

Please translate the following sentences into Chinese and read them aloud.

1. Wish you happy birthday!
2. This is a Korean dish I cooked.
3. That is a cake she bought.
4. So beautiful a towel?
5. That expensive?
6. Have food first and then have some fruit.
7. This year I'll go to USA first and then go to Hongkong.
8. His computer is the same as mine.

Assignment II

Please use your own background to complete the following dialogues.

1. A：你来了中国以后去旅游了吗？

   B：____________________________。

2. A：您的生日是几月几号？

   B：________________________。

3. A：你过生日的时候吃蛋糕吗？

   B：________________________。

4. A：你觉得在中国过生日跟在美国一样吗？

   B：________________________。

5. A：朋友过生日的时候,你送礼物吗？

   B：________________________。

Dì shíyī kè

第十一课

Wǒ yào yóupiào

我 要 邮票

Language Points

a. 我要红毛衣。
b. 我要一杯啤酒。
c. 我想买笔记本电脑。

Text

(In the office)

	Shǐmìsī xiānsheng, nín zài zhǎo shénme?
秘　书：	史密斯　先生，　您　在　找　什么？
	Wǒ zài zhǎo yóupiào ne.
史密斯：	我　在　找　邮票　呢。
	Wǒ zhèr yǒu yóupiào. Yǒu bāmáo de hé liùmáode,
秘　书：	我　这儿　有　邮票。有　八毛　的　和　六毛的，
	nín yào nǎ yī zhǒng?
	您　要　哪　一　种？
	Wǒ yào liùmáo de, liǎng zhāng. Bùguò, hái yào
史密斯：	我　要　六毛　的，　两　张。　不过，　还　要
	yīzhāng wǔkuài sìmáo de, nǐ yǒu ma?
	一张　五块　四毛　的，　你　有　吗？
	Méiyǒu. Nín xiǎng jì wǎng Měiguó, duì ma?
秘　书：	没有。　您　想　寄　往　美国，　对　吗？
	Duì.
史密斯：	对。
	Nà wǒ xiànzài jiù qù yóujú mǎi.
秘　书：	那　我　现在　就　去　邮局　买。
	Xièxie!
史密斯：	谢谢！

Words

1. 红	hóng	(adj.)	red
2. 杯	bēi	(cl.)	(used of things contained in cups)
3. 笔记本	bǐjìběn	(n.)	notebook
4. 邮票	yóupiào	(n.)	postage stamp
5. 毛	máo	(cl.,n.)	unit of money smaller than *yuan*

6. 种	zhǒng	(cl.)	kind, type
7. 块	kuài	(n.,cl.)	unit of money the same as *yuan*
8. 想	xiǎng	(adj.)	desired
9. 往	wǎng	(prep.)	(expressing the direction of an action)

Proper nouns

(一)

1. 法国 Fǎguó

(二)

1. 麦当劳 Màidāngláo
2. 肯德基 Kěndéjī

Supplementary words

1. 帽子	màozi	(n.)	cap
2. 绿	lǜ	(adj.)	green
3. 苹果	píngguǒ	(n.)	apple
4. 橘子	júzi	(n.)	orange
5. 汽车	qìchē	(n.)	vehicle
6. 开	kāi	(v.)	run (compnany)
7. 票	piào	(n.)	ticket
8. 告诉	gàosu	(v.)	tell
9. 坐	zuò	(v.)	take
10. 飞机	fēijī	(n.)	plane
11. 杂技	zájì	(n.)	acrobatics
12. 葡萄酒	pútaojiǔ	(n.)	wine
13. 烧烤	shāokǎo	(n.)	barbecue
14. 京剧 京戏	jīngjù jīngxì	(n.)	Beijing Opera

Grammatical explanation

一、“要”＋ noun

The Chinese word“要”has three meanings：

1. want
2. want to do
3. must do

In the first case the word is followed by noun，while in the second and third cases the word is followed by verbs. Let's first look at the examples with the word of “want”.

(1)我要苹果。　　(I want some apples.)
(2)你要什么？　　(What do you want?)
(3)我要笔记本。　　(I want a notebook.)

二、“要”＋ verb and“想”＋ verb

In the second case where “要” means “want to do”，the Chinese word“想” can be used instead of “要” and the meaning remains the same.

(1)史密斯先生要坐飞机。(Mr. Smith wants to take plane.)
(2)我要喝一杯咖啡。　　(I want to drink a cup of coffee.)
(3)你想吃什么？　　(What do you want to eat?)

♣Note：

The negation form of both patterns are “不想” ＋ verb，while “不要”＋ verb has the meaning of “mustn't do”.

(1)我不想看杂技。　　(I don't want to watch acrobatics.)
(2)他们不想一起去。　　(They don't want to go together.)

三、“的” in“我要六毛的”

The“的”introduced in Lesson Two means possession. For example：

(1)我的帽子　　(my cap)
(2)这是你的汽车吗？　　(Is this your car?)

In addition，it can also be used to indicate a relation of modification. For example：

(1)便宜的帽子　　(inexpensive cap)
(2)快乐的生日　　(happy birthday)
(3)便宜的　　(the inexpensive)

(4)好吃的　　(the delicious)
(5)红的　　(the red)

四、The ways of expressing the concepts of money

The basic unit of Chinese currency is “元”, which is called “块” in colloquial Chinese. One-tenth of “块” is “毛”; one-tenth of “毛” is “分”.

Exercise I

Please read aloud the following sentences.

1. ① 我要六毛的,两张。
② 我要红毛衣。
③ 她要帽子。
④ 我要绿茶,他要咖啡。
⑤ 小张要苹果,我要橘子。

2. ① 我要买笔记本电脑。
② 我要买汽车。
③ 江先生要开公司。
④ 她要去美国。
⑤ 史密斯太太要来上海。

3. ① 我想买笔记本电脑。
② 我想买汽车。
③ 江先生想开公司。
④ 她想去美国。
⑤ 史密斯太太想来上海。

4. ① 那我现在就去买。
② 那我马上告诉他。
③ 那我就坐飞机。
④ 那我不干了。
⑤ 那我不买了。

5. 史密斯先生在找邮票，对吗？→ 对，他在找邮票。
   ① 你要红毛衣，对吗？
   ② 你想买汽车，对吗？
   ③ 江先生想开公司，对吗？
   ④ 她想去美国，对吗？
   ⑤ 史密斯太太想来上海，对吗？

6. 史密斯先生在找邮票，对吗？→ 不，他没在找邮票。
   ① 你要红毛衣，对吗？
   ② 你想买汽车，对吗？
   ③ 江先生想开公司，对吗？
   ④ 她想去美国，对吗？
   ⑤ 史密斯太太想来上海，对吗？

Exercise II

Please practice reading the following dialogues.

1. A：我这儿有邮票，有八毛的和六毛的，您要哪一种？
   B：我要六毛的，两张。
   ① 杂技票　　五十块的和一百二十块的　　一百二十块
   ② 京剧票　　八十块的和一百五十块的　　八十块

2. A：您想寄往美国，对吗？
   B：对。
   ① 吃法国菜　　不，我不想吃法国菜
   ② 喝葡萄酒　　对，我想喝葡萄酒

3. A：你想不想吃麦当劳？
   B：想吃。你呢？
   A：我也想吃。
   ①肯德基　　②烧烤

Assignment I

Please translate the following sentences into Chinese and read them aloud.

1. What do you want when you come to China?
2. What do you want to do now?
3. Do you want to drink Chinese wine?
4. Do you want to return to USA?
5. Do you want to go abroad to study in China?
6. Do you want to have a stroll on the pedestrian street with your friends?
7. Do you often want to drink tea when you are at work?
8. I have some American magazines there. Do you want to read them?

Assignment II

Please use your own background to complete the following dialogues.

1. A：现在，你想买什么？

   B：________________________________。

2. A：你想在中国旅游吗？想去哪儿？

   B：________________________________。

3. A：你想去中国朋友家玩儿吗？

   B：________________________________。

4. A：您想在中国工作吗？

   B：________________________________。

5. A：休息天，您想不想看中国电影？

   B：________________________________。

Dì shíèr kè
第十二课

Zài xuéxiào
在 学校

Language Points

a. 逛马路很有意思。
b. 大的好吃,小的不好吃。
c. 学习紧张没办法,有时间再玩儿吧。
d. 忙是好事。

Text

Huáng lǎoshī, hǎojiǔ bù jiàn le!
史密斯：黄 老师，好久 不 见 了！

Hǎojiǔ bù jiàn le, Shǐmìsī xiānsheng!
黄老师：好久 不 见 了，史密斯 先生！

Huáng lǎoshī, shànggeyuè wǒ gōngzuò tài máng le, qǐngjià hěn duō, zhēn duìbuqǐ!
史密斯：黄 老师，上个月 我 工作 太 忙 了，请假 很 多，真 对不起！

Gōngzuò máng méi bànfǎ, yǒu kòngr de shíhou zhuājǐn xuéxí ba.
黄老师：工作 忙 没 办法，有 空儿 的 时候 抓紧 学习 吧。

Míngbai le. Lǎoshī, shàngcì de zuòyè wǒ yǐjing zuòhǎo le.
史密斯：明白 了。老师，上次 的 作业 我 已经 做好 了。

Shì ma? Nà wǒmen xiān kàn nín de zuòyè ba.
黄老师：是 吗？那 我们 先 看 您 的 作业 吧。

Hǎo.
史密斯：好。

……

Shǐmìsī xiānsheng, miànbāo de "bāo" zì nín xiě cuò le, nín xiě de shì Rìyǔ de "bāo" zì ba.
黄老师：史密斯 先生，面包 的 "包" 字 您 写 错 了，您 写 的 是 日语 的 "包" 字 吧。

Āiyā, zhēnde! Wǒ chóng xiě yī biàn.
史密斯：哎呀，真的！我 重 写 一 遍。

Qítā dōu hěn hǎo.
黄老师：其他 都 很 好。

Xièxie!
史密斯： 谢谢！

Xiàmian, wǒmen xuéxí dì shíwǔ kè……
黄老师： 下面， 我们 学习 第 十五 课……

Words

1. 有意思	yǒuyìsi	(adj.)	interesting
2. 紧张	jǐnzhāng	(adj.)	busy
3. 办法	bànfǎ	(n.)	method
4. 再	zài	(adv.)	again
5. 吧	ba	(aux.)	(used at the end of a sentence) indicating suggestion, etc
6. 上(个)月	shàng(ge)yuè	(n.)	last month
7. 请假	qǐngjià		ask for a leave
8. 多	duō	(adj.)	many, much
9. 抓紧	zhuājǐn	(v.)	lose no time
10. 上次	shàngcì	(n.)	last time
11. 作业	zuòyè	(n.)	assignment
12. 已经	yǐjing	(adv.)	already
13. 面包	miànbāo	(n.)	bread
14. 字	zì	(n.)	character
15. 写	xiě	(v.)	write
16. 错	cuò	(adj., n.)	incorrect, mistake
17. 日语	rìyǔ	(n.)	Japanese
日文	rìwén		
18. 哎呀	āiyā	(int.)	lumme
19. 真的	zhēnde		really
20. 重	chóng	(adv.)	again
21. 遍	biàn	(cl.)	time
22. 其他	qítā	(pron.)	other
23. 课	kè	(cl.)	(of textbook) lesson
24. 下面	xiàmian	(n.)	following

Supplementary words

1. 贵	guì	(adj.)	expensive
2. 身体	shēntǐ	(n.)	body
3. 没关系	méiguānxi		It doesn't matter.
4. 事	shì	(n.)	affair, thing
5. 安静	ānjìng	(adj.)	quiet
6. 年轻	niánqīng	(adj.)	young
7. 力气	lìqi	(n.)	strength
8. 缺席	quēxí	(v.)	be absent
9. 排球	páiqiú	(n.)	volleyball

Grammatical explanation

一、"Verb" or "verb + object" used as subject

The subject of a sentence is not confined to such simple nouns as "我", "你", "狗", and "猫". A structure as complex as a sentence can also be used as the subject (or topic). Some types of these will be introduced in this lesson.

First come the cases where the subject includes a verb.

(1)看中国电影很有意思。
(To watch Chinese movies is very interesting.)

(2)大家一起吃饭真热闹。
(It is hilarious that all of us have dinner together.)

二、Subject with "的"

Such phrases as "我的" and "你的" introduced in Lesson Two can be followed by concrete content to form "我的…" and "你的…". If they are not followed by anything, they correspond to "mine" and "yours" in English.

"的" can also be used after adjectives to mean "adjective + thing/person". Thus adjectives become nouns and can be used as subjects. For example:

(1)好吃的是这个。 (The delicious is this.)

(2)年轻的有力气。 (The young are forceful.)

(3)漂亮的很贵。 (The beautiful are expensive.)

The structure with "的" after verb means "person or thing that has done ...". For example:

(1)你吃的是我的点心。(What you have eaten is my cake.)

(2)你学的是什么? (What is what you have learned? /What have you learned?)

三、"Subject + predicate" used as subject

A sentence may be used as a subject, as is the case with the English language. For example:

(1)你做作业非常好。 (That you have done your homework is very good.)

(2)东西贵没有人买。 (People do not buy those things which are expensive.)

(3)她不来没办法。 (There is no way out that she won't come.)

四、"Adjectives" used as subject

In Chinese adjectives can be directly used as subjects, which is different from that in English where an adjective should be preceded by a definite article "the".

(1)太干净也不好。 (To be too clean is no good.)

(2)忙是好事。 (Being busy is good)

五、Verb + "好"

The Chinese word "好" means "good". Verbs followed by "好" change into "compound verbs", which mean the completion of actions.

The Chinese word "错" means "incorrect". Verbs followed by "错" mean "to do something incorrectly", such as "读错" meaning "mispronounce" and "写错" meaning "write incorrectly".

The Chinese word "完" means "completion".

These compound verbs mean the completion of actions and they are often used together with "了" in simple sentences. For example:

(1)看好了。 (Watching is over.)

(2)听错了。 (The listening is inaccurate.)

(3)唱完了。　　　　　　(The singing is over.)

Exercise I

Please read aloud the following sentences.

1. ① 请假很多。
② 逛马路很有意思。
③ 学汉语很难。
④ 见朋友很高兴。
⑤ 找东西太麻烦了。

2. ① 你写的是日文的"包"字吧。
② 大的好吃,小的不好吃。
③ 我买的贵,她买的便宜。
④ 来的是上海人,去的是北京人。
⑤ 红的漂亮,黄的不漂亮。

3. ① 工作忙没办法。
② 学习紧张没办法。
③ 身体好很重要。
④ 你不去没关系。
⑤ 她做饭很快。

4. ① 忙是好事。
② 太热闹不好,太安静也不好。
③ 年轻有力气。

5. 例:老师,上次的作业我已经做好了。→ 是吗?
① 科长,今天的工作我已经做好了。
② 史密斯先生,晚饭我已经做好了。
③ 妈妈,房间我已经打扫好了。

6. 例:那我们先看你的作业吧。→ 好。
① 那我们先休息吧。
② 那你们先下班吧。

③ 那我们先吃吧。

Exercise II

Please practice reading the following dialogues.

1. A：黄老师，上个月我工作太忙了，请假很多，真对不起！
   B：工作忙没办法，有空儿的时候抓紧学习吧。
   ① 休息　　练习　　　② 缺席　　学

2. A：老师，上次的作业我已经做好了。
   B：是吗？那我们先看你的作业吧。
   ① 科长　　　　今天的工作　　你先回家
   ② 史密斯先生　晚饭　　　　　我们先吃

3. A：史密斯先生，面包的"包"字你写错了。
   B：哎呀，真的！
   ① 八十的"八"　　说
   ② 排球的"排"　　读

Assignment I

Please translate the following sentences into Chinese and read them aloud.

1. To do Chinese homework is not difficult.
2. To cook Korean dishes is very interesting.
3. Is this the book that you want?
4. What I bought are these clothes?
5. Are the big delicious?
6. The flight ticket has been bought.
7. Today's work has been finished.
8. You have done this assignment incorrectly.

Assignment II

Please use your own background to complete the following dialogues.

1. A：你在学汉语吗？

   B：______________________________。

2. A：你工作忙的时候也学汉语吗？请假多吗？

   B：______________________________。

3. A：学汉语难吗？

   B：______________________________。

4. A：你经常做汉语作业吗？

   B：______________________________。

5. A：你经常说汉语吗？

   B：______________________________。

Dì shísān kè
第十三课

Guò jié
过节

Language Points

a. 我干什么好呢？
b. 咱们去豫园，还是去步行街？
c. 我去过大连。

Text

Jīntiān shì "Wǔ-Yī" Guójì Láodòngjié, jiēshang rén zhēn duō a!
史密斯：今天是"五一"国际劳动节，街上人真多啊！

Shì a, wǒmen qù nǎli wánr hǎo ne?
卡森先生：是啊，我们去哪里玩儿好呢？

Qù guàng Nánjīngxīlù, háishi qù kàn diànyǐng?
卡森太太：去逛南京西路，还是去看电影？

Háishi qù kàn diànyǐng ba.
江先生：还是去看电影吧。

Hǎo wa! Lái Shànghǎi yǐhòu, wǒ hái méi kànguo Zhōngguó diànyǐng ne.
史密斯：好哇！来上海以后，我还没看过中国电影呢。

Shì ma? Wǒ hé xiānsheng yǐjīng kànguo liǎngcì le.
卡森太太：是吗？我和先生已经看过两次了。

Zhēnde? Háishi hé tàitai zài yīqǐ hǎo wa!
史密斯：真的？还是和太太在一起好哇！

Xiànzài, zánmen jiù qù diànyǐngyuàn, kànwán diànyǐng yǐhòu yīqǐ chī wǎnfàn, zěnmeyàng?
江先生：现在，咱们就去电影院，看完电影以后一起吃晚饭，怎么样？

Wǒ tóngyì! Jīntiān shì jiérì, wǎnshang wǒmen hǎohāor hē yī bēi ba.
史密斯：我同意！今天是节日，晚上我们好好儿喝一杯吧。

Hǎo!
卡森夫妇：好！

Words

1. 过	guo	(aux.)	(indicating past actions)
2. 咱们	zánmen	(pron.)	we
3. 还是	háishi	(conj.)	or
4. 节	jié	(n.)	festival
5. 两	liǎng	(num.)	two
6. 还是	háishi	(adv.)	had better
7. 一起	yīqǐ	(adv.)	together
8. 电影院	diànyǐngyuàn	(n.)	cinema
9. 晚饭	wǎnfàn	(n.)	supper
10. 同意	tóngyì	(v.)	agree
11. 节日	jiérì	(n.)	festival

Proper nouns

(一)

1. 豫园　Yùyuán
2. 南京西路　Nánjīngxīlù
3. 淮海路　Huáihǎilù
4. 新天地　Xīntiāndì

(二)

1. 大连　Dàlián
2. 旧金山　Jiùjīnshān

(三)

1. 上海大剧院　Shànghǎi Dàjùyuàn
2. 上海博物馆　Shànghǎi Bówùguǎn
3. 上海书城　Shànghǎi Shūchéng

Supplementary words

1. 可乐	kělè	(n.)	cola
2. 橙汁	chéngzhī	(n.)	orange juice

3. 忌司	jìsī	(n.)	cheese
4. 巧克力	qiǎokèlì	(n.)	chocolate
5. 卡拉 OK	kǎlā'ōukèi	(n.)	Karaoke
6. 点心	diǎnxīn	(n.)	dim sum
7. 音乐	yīnyuè	(n.)	music
8. 国宝	guóbǎo	(n.)	national treasure
9. 展览	zhǎnlǎn	(n.)	exhibition
10. 会	huì	(n.)	party, gathering
11. 累	lèi	(v.)	be tired
12. 方便	fāngbiàn	(adj.)	convenient

Grammatical explanation

一、Verb ＋"过"

The Chinese word "过" means experience, i. e. "have done or did something". For example:

(1)我去过上海书城。 (I have been to Shanghai Book City.)

(2)你打过高尔夫吗? (Did you play golf?)

The negation form is the structure "没(有) ＋ verb ＋ 过". For example:

她没有去过美国。 (She has not been to USA.)

二、"…好呢?"

The Chinese word "好" means good and "呢" indicates a question. The structure "…好呢?" is used to ask "Is it good to do something under certain conditions". But in translating this structure into English, flexibility should be observed according to the concrete contexts. For example:

(1)买什么好呢? (What shall I buy?)

(2)星期天我们去哪里玩儿好呢? (Where shall we go for a visit on Sunday?)

三、"还是"

The structure "还是" has two meanings.

① "…还是…?"

This structure is used in a question to put two possibilities together for listeners to make a choice. Here "还是" can be translated into "or". For example:

(1)这是你的，还是他的？(Is this yours or his?)

(2)你喝咖啡，还是喝红茶？(Which would you like to drink, coffee or black tea?)

②"还是…"

The structure "还是" also has the meaning of comparison. But here it is not used in a question and the object of comparison is not definite. It roughly means "had better". For example:

(1)还是这个好。(Still this is better.)

(2)我们还是去北京吧。(We'd better go to Beijing.)

四、The distinction between "两" and "二"

Generally speaking, the word "两" is used to express "number" and "times" while "二" is used to express order. Nevertheless there are still exceptions. For example, in expressing points of time, "两点" is used instead of "二点".

(1)我去过两次中国。(I've been to China for twice.)

(2)我们今天学习第二课。(We will learn Lesson Two today.)

Exercise I

Please read aloud the following sentences.

1. ① 我们去哪里玩儿好呢？
② 我干什么好呢？
③ 你吃什么好呢？
④ 我们什么时候去好呢？
⑤ 你们什么时候休息好呢？

2. ① 去逛南京西路，还是去看电影？
② 咱们去豫园，还是去步行街？
③ 她喝可乐，还是喝橙汁？
④ 你的朋友喜欢华盛顿，还是旧金山？

⑤ 你买忌司蛋糕，还是巧克力蛋糕？

3. ① 我和先生已经看过两次了。
② 我去过大连。
③ 他们去过淮海路的卡拉 OK 店。
④ 他吃过上海的点心。
⑤ 史密斯先生和朋友一起看过中国电影。

4. ① 还是和太太在一起好哇！
② 还是在中国工作好哇！
③ 还是来上海留学好。
④ 还是学英语有意思。
⑤ 还是有手机方便。

5. 例：史密斯先生和朋友去看电影了吗？→ 是的，他和大家去看电影了。
① 他们去过淮海路的卡拉 OK 店吗？
② 他吃过上海的点心吗？
③ 史密斯先生和朋友一起喝过酒吗？

6. 例：史密斯先生和朋友去逛街了吗？→ 没有，史密斯先生没和朋友去逛街。
① 他们去过淮海路的卡拉 OK 店吗？
② 他吃过上海的点心吗？
③ 史密斯先生和朋友一起喝过酒吗？

Exercise II

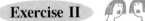

Please practice reading the following dialogues.

1. A：还是去看电影吧。
B：好哇！来上海以后，我还没看过中国电影呢。
① 听音乐会　　　去过上海大剧院
② 看国宝展览　　去过上海博物馆

2. A：现在，咱们就去电影院，看完电影以后一起去吃晚饭，怎么样？
   B：我同意！
   ① 上海书城　　买完书
   ② 新天地　　逛完新天地

3. A：我和小王去逛街，你去，还是不去？
   B：不去。因为我感冒了。
   ① 没空儿　　② 累了

4. A：豫园你去过没去过？
   B：没有。
   A：那明天我们一起去，怎么样？
   B：好。
   ① 上海菜　　吃
   ② 美国音乐　　听

Assignment I

Please translate the following sentences into Chinese and read them aloud.

1. Will you go back to USA or travel in China during the May Day holiday this year?
2. Which would you like, cheese cake or chocolate cake?
3. Tomorrow we will be free. Where shall we go to have our meals?
4. What TV program shall we watch now?
5. Have you been to USA?
6. After I came to Shanghai, I've been to Shanghai Grand Theatre.
7. It is still better to buy laptop.
8. It is still more interesting to watch movies.

Assignment II

Please use your own background to complete the following dialogues.

1. A：你在中国过过节日吗？
   B：________________________________。

2. A：你喜欢在中国过节吗？

   B：______________________________________。

3. A：你去过上海的哪些地方？

   B：______________________________________。

4. A：学汉语难，还是学英语难？

   B：______________________________________。

5. A：休息天，你经常和朋友一起喝酒，还是打高尔夫？

   B：______________________________________。

Dì shísì kè

第十四课

Zuò dìtiě qù chīfàn

坐 地铁 去 吃饭

Language Points

a. 我一边听音乐，一边看杂志。
b. 下星期一，我得去南京出差。
c. 请看一下儿。

Text

(Coming out of the cinema)

Jīntiān de diànyǐng zhēn yǒuqù!
卡森太太：今天 的 电影 真 有趣！

Ǹg. Shǐmìsī, nǐ dōu kàndǒng le ma?
卡森先生：嗯。(To Smith)史密斯，你 都 看懂 了 吗？

Méiyǒu! Zhǐ kàndǒng le yīdiǎnr. Wǒ yībiān kàn,
史 密 斯：没有！ 只 看懂 了 一点儿。我 一边 看，
yībiān wèn Jiāng xiānsheng. Jiāng
一边 问 江 先生。 (To Mr. Jiang) 江
xiānsheng, kàn diànyǐng de shíhou dǎrǎo nǐ le,
先生， 看 电影 的 时候 打扰 你 了，
zhēn duìbuqǐ!
真 对不起！

Méiguānxi. Xiànzài, wǒmen zuò dìtiě yīhàoxiàn
江 先 生：没关系。 现在， 我们 坐 地铁 一号线
qù Xújiāhuì chīfàn ba.
去 徐家汇 吃饭 吧。

史 密 斯：Hǎo!
卡森夫妇：好！

(Arriving at subway station)

Wǒ yǒu jiāotōngkǎ, nǐmen ne?
江 先 生：我 有 交通卡， 你们 呢？

Wǒmen yě yǒu.
卡森夫妇：我们 也 有。

Wǒ méiyǒu. Děi qù zìdòng shòupiàojī nàr
史 密 斯：我 没有。 得 去 自动 售票机 那儿
mǎi piào. Qǐng nǐmen děng wǒ yīxiàr.
买 票。 请 你们 等 我 一下儿。

江 先 生：Hǎo!
卡森夫妇：好！

Words

1. 一边…一边…	yībiān…yībiān…		while
2. 下星期	xiàxīngqī	(n.)	next week
3. 得	děi	(aux.,v.)	have to
4. 出差	chūchāi	(v.)	go on errands
5. 一下儿	yīxiàr		a moment
6. 坐	zuò	(v.)	take
7. 地铁	dìtiě	(n.)	subway
8. 有趣	yǒuqù	(adj.)	interesting
9. 嗯	ǹg	(int.)	er
10. 懂	dǒng	(v.)	understand
11. 只	zhǐ	(adv.)	only
12. 打扰	dǎrǎo	(v.)	bother
13. 一号线	yīhàoxiàn	(n.)	Line No. 1
14. 交通	jiāotōng	(n.)	traffic
15. 自动	zìdòng	(n.)	automatic
16. 售票机	shòupiàojī	(n.)	ticket machine

Proper nouns

1. 徐家汇	Xújiāhuì
2. 明珠线	Míngzhūxiàn

Supplementary words

1. 工作	gōngzuò	(v.,n.)	work
2. 聊天儿	liáotiānr	(v.,n.)	chat
3. 搬	bān	(v.)	move
4. 考试	kǎoshì	(v.,n.)	test
5. 衬衫	chènshān	(n.)	shirt
6. 每天	měitiān	(n.)	every day
7. 公共汽车	gōnggòngqìchē	(n.)	bus

8. 出租车	chūzūchē	(n.)	taxi
9. 二号线	èrhàoxiàn	(n.)	Line No. 2
10. 售票处	shòupiàochù	(n.)	ticket office
11. 窗口	chuāngkǒu	(n.)	wicket
12. DVD		(n.)	DVD

Grammatical explanation

一、"都…了"

The Chinese word "都" generally means "all". But as a special usage, it also means "already" or "completely". For example:

(1)那本书都看完了。 (I've already finished reading that book.)

(2)我们都做了。 (We've done all things.)

二、"一边…一边…"

The structure "一边…一边…" means "at the same time" or "while". For example:

(1)一边听音乐,一边看小说。(read novels while listening to music)

(2)一边吃饭,一边聊天儿。 (chat while having dinner)

三、"得 + verb"

In Lesson Eleven we have introduced such auxiliary verbs as "要" and "想". In this lesson another one will be introduced, that is, "得". It is used before verbs with the meaning of "have to" or "must". What deserves special attention is that "得" as a notional verb is pronounced "dé", which means "get". For example:

(1)现在我得去医院。 (Now I have to go to the hospital.)

(2)你得买什么? (What must you buy?)

四、"…一下儿"

The structure "…一下儿" is used after verb with the meaning of "a little" or "a bit". For example:

(1)看一下儿。 (Take a look.)

(2)听一下儿。 (Listen to something.)

五、“去” + noun + “那儿” + verb (verb + object)

The word “去” is normally followed by a noun of place, e.g. “去上海”. What if the nouns of place are replaced by nouns of persons (things) or pronouns? In Chinese language such expressions as “去他” and “去自动售票机” are not acceptable. The expression “那儿” is added after nouns or pronouns to change them into nouns of place. If the person (thing) is close to the speaker, the expression “这儿” can be used instead. For example:

(1)来我这儿坐吧。 (Come to me to take a seat.)
(2)你什么时候去老师那儿?(When will you go to the teacher?)

Exercise I

Please read aloud the following sentences.

1. ① 你都看懂了吗?
   ② 你都听懂了吗?
   ③ 你都说了吗?
   ④ 他们都走了吗?
   ⑤ 你们都买了吗?

2. ① 只看懂一点儿。
   ② 只学了一点儿。
   ③ 只买了一点儿。
   ④ 只做了一点儿。
   ⑤ 只喝了一点儿。

3. ① 我一边看,一边问江先生。
   ② 我一边听音乐,一边看杂志。
   ③ 史密斯先生一边工作,一边学习汉语。
   ④ 她们一边聊天儿,一边吃点心。
   ⑤ 他一边坐地铁,一边看报纸。

4. ① 我得去自动售票机那儿买票。
   ② 下星期一,我得去南京出差。
   ③ 明年,我得搬家。

④ 下个月，我们得考试。
⑤ 天暖和了，我得买两件衬衫。

5. 例：史密斯先生和大家坐地铁去吃饭吗？→ 对，史密斯先生和大家坐地铁去吃饭。
① 他每天坐公共汽车上班吗？
② 你坐出租车回家吗？
③ 黄老师坐地铁二号线去浦东吗？

6. 例：史密斯先生和大家坐出租车去吃饭吗？→ 没有，史密斯先生和大家没坐出租车去吃饭。
① 他坐公共汽车上班吗？
② 你坐出租车回家吗？
③ 黄老师坐地铁二号线去浦东吗？

Exercise II

Please practice reading the following dialogues.

1. A：现在，我们坐<u>地铁一号线</u>去<u>淮海路</u>吃饭吧。
B：好！
① 地铁二号线　　南京西路
② 明珠线　　徐家汇

2. A：我得去<u>自动售票机那儿</u>买票。请你们等我一下儿。
B：好！
①售票处　　②窗口

3. A：喂，小张，你在干什么？
B：我在看 VCD。
A：我去你房间玩儿好吗？
B：好哇。我们一边看，一边<u>喝茶</u>吧。
①吃点心　　②喝咖啡

Assignment I

Please translate the following sentences into Chinese and read them aloud.

1. How interesting the book is!
2. I often watch TV while I'm having dinner in the evening.
3. Mrs. Carsen is now listening to music while she is cleaning the room.
4. Xiao Wang and I went to the museum together by bus this afternoon.
5. After work this afternoon I'll take subway to go shopping in West Nanjing Road.
6. Next week we'll be very busy, so we have to work on Sunday.
7. Tomorrow I have to go back to USA on business, so I cannot attend class.
8. Excuse me, but I'll place a telephone call. Please wait for a while.

Assignment II

Please use your own background to complete the following dialogues.

1. A：来中国以后，你一边工作，一边学习汉语吗？

   B：________________________________。

2. A：你每天坐什么去上班？

   B：________________________________。

3. A：你坐过上海的地铁吗？

   B：________________________________。

4. A：你有交通卡吗？

   B：________________________________。

5. A：星期天，你得去哪儿？

   B：________________________________。

Dì shíwǔ kè

第十五课

Zuò kè

做客

Language Points

a. 今天我来洗碗。
b. 你多大了？
c. 这儿热闹极了。

Text

(In the house of Mr. Jiang)

	Shǐmìsī xiānsheng, wǒ lái jièshào yīxiàr, zhè
江先生：	史密斯 先生， 我 来 介绍 一下儿，这
	shì wǒbàba, zhè shì wǒ māma.
	是 我爸爸， 这 是 我 妈妈。
	nǐ hǎo! Huānyíng, huānyíng.
江先生父母：	你 好！ 欢迎， 欢迎。
	Bófù、 bómǔ, nǐmen hǎo!
史密斯：	伯父、 伯母， 你们 好！
	Shūshu, nǐ shì Měiguó shūshu ma?
文文：	叔叔， 你 是 美国 叔叔 吗？
	Zhè shì wǒ de nǚ'ér. Wénwen,
江先生：	这 是 我 的 女儿。(To his daughter) 文文，
	nǐ děi xiān shuō "shūshu nín hǎo!".
	你 得 先 说 "叔叔 您 好！"。
	Shūshu, nín hǎo!
文文：	叔叔， 您 好！
	Nǐ hǎo! Duō dà le?
史密斯：	你 好！多 大 了？
	Bā suì le.
文文：	八 岁 了。
	Lái, zhè shì gěi nǐ de xiǎo lǐwù.
史密斯：	来， 这 是 给 你 的 小 礼物。
	Xièxie shūshu!
文文：	谢谢 叔叔！
	Wénwen kě'ài jíle!
史密斯：	文文 可爱 极了！
	Shǐmìsī xiānsheng, qǐng hē chá.
江夫人：	史密斯 先生， 请 喝 茶。
	Xièxie, Jiāng fūrén!
史密斯：	谢谢， 江 夫人！

Shǐmìsī xiānsheng, nín jīntiān zài wǒ jiā
江夫人： 史密斯 先生， 您 今天 在 我 家
chī wǔfàn ba.
吃 午饭 吧。

Zhēn bùhǎoyìsi. Tiān máfan le!
史密斯： 真 不好意思。 添 麻烦 了！

Words

1. 来	lái		indicating purpose
2. 碗	wǎn	(n.)	bowl
3. 多	duō	(adv.)	how (old)
4. …极了	…jíle		extemely
5. 做客	zuòkè		be a guest
6. 介绍	jièshào	(v.)	introduce
7. 爸爸	bàba	(n.)	father
8. 妈妈	māma	(n.)	mother
9. 父母	fùmǔ	(n.)	parent
10. 欢迎	huānyíng	(v.)	welcome
11. 伯父/伯伯	bófù/bóbo	(n.)	uncle
12. 伯母	bómǔ	(n.)	aunt
13. 叔叔	shūshu	(n.)	uncle (father's friends who are younger)
14. 女儿	nǚ'ér	(n.)	daughter
15. 岁	suì	(cl.)	(of age)
16. 可爱	kě'ài	(adj.)	lovely
17. 给	gěi	(v.)	give
18. 午饭	wǔfàn	(n.)	lunch
19. 不好意思	bùhǎoyìsi		I'm sorry (to bother you).
20. 添	tiān	(v.)	bother
21. 麻烦	máfan	(v.,adj.)	trouble

Proper nouns

文文　Wénwen

Supplementary words

1. 弟弟	dìdi	(n.)	younger brother
2. 妹妹	mèimei	(n.)	younger sister
3. 走	zǒu	(v.)	walk
4. 久	jiǔ	(adj.)	long (time)
5. 长	cháng	(adj.)	long (time)
6. 双	shuāng	(cl.)	(used of things in pair)
7. 鞋	xié	(n.)	shoe
8. 饺子	jiǎozi	(n.)	jiaozi
9. 顿	dùn	(cl.)	(used of meals)
10. 便饭	biànfàn	(n.)	a simple meal

Grammatical explanation

一、"来" + verb

The word "来" means "to come". When it is used before verbs, it means "to do ..." "actively" or "on one's own initiative". For example:

(1)我来给你做饭。　(Let me cook for you.)

(2)我来给你寄行李。　(Let me send the luggage for you.)

二、Questions with the adverb "多"

The word "多" means "many" or "much". But it can also be used in a question to ask about the degree. For example:

(1)南浦大桥多长？　(How long is the Nanpu Bridge?)

(2)东方明珠电视塔多高？(How high is the Oriental Pearl TV Tower?)

三、"…极了"

This structure is similar to such words and expressions as "很", "非常", and "太…了", indicating degree. But the former indicates a degree higher than that indicated by the latter ones. For example:

(1)从这儿去方便极了。 (It is tremendously convenient to leave from this place.)

(2)这本书好极了。 (This book is considerably good.)

四、Words addressing family members

Here is a summary of words addressing family members.

爷爷 yéye
(grandfather)
奶奶 nǎinai
(grandmother)
爸爸 bàba
(father)
妈妈 māma
(mother)
哥哥 gēge
(elder brother)
姐姐 jiějie
(elder sister)
弟弟 dìdi
(younger brother)
妹妹 mèimei
(younger sister)

Exercise I

Please read aloud the following sentences.

1. ① 我来介绍一下儿,这是我爸爸,这是我妈妈。
② 我来介绍一下儿,这是我哥哥,这是我弟弟。
③ 我来介绍一下儿,这是我姐姐,这是我妹妹。
④ 我来介绍一下儿,这是我朋友。
⑤ 我来介绍一下儿,这是我先生。

2. ① 你得先说叔叔您好!
② 你得先说对不起。
③ 她得先休息。
④ 我们得先吃饭。
⑤ 你们得先走。

3. ① 你多大了?
② 你在上海多久了?
③ 你女儿多高了?
④ 这件衣服多长?

⑤ 那双鞋多大?

4. ① 文文可爱极了!
② 笔记本电脑贵极了!
③ 昨天的电影有趣极了!
④ 今天,我忙极了!
⑤ 美国点心好吃极了!

5. 例:史密斯先生去江先生家做客了?→ 对,史密斯先生去江先生家做客了。
① 你去学校见黄老师了?
② 小张去她家玩儿了?
③ 他们去饭店吃饭了?

6. 例:史密斯先生给文文小礼物了?→ 是的,史密斯先生给文文小礼物了。
① 你给朋友生日礼物了?
② 他给妹妹杂志了?
③ 小王给你信了?

Exercise II

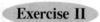

Please practice reading the following dialogues.

1. A:我来介绍一下儿,这是我爸爸,这是我妈妈。
B:你好! 欢迎,欢迎。
C:你们好!
① 这是我男朋友　　您好
② 这是我女朋友　　你好

2. A:你好! 多大了?
B:八岁了。
① 五岁　　② 十岁

3. A:史密斯先生,今天在我家吃午饭吧。

B：真不好意思。添麻烦了！
① 吃点儿饺子　　② 吃顿便饭

Assignment I

Please translate the following sentences into Chinese and read them aloud.

1. Let me make an introduction. This is our general manager and these are his friends.
2. Let me clean the room today.
3. You do this work, please.
4. His daughter is very beautiful.
5. Mr. Jiang's daughter is very lovely.
6. We are very busy with our work.
7. How long is the pedestrian street?
8. How high is this building?

Assignment II

Please use your own background to complete the following dialogues.

1. A：在中国的时候，你去中国朋友家做过客吗？
   B：________________________________。
2. A：你想去中国朋友家做客吗？
   B：________________________________。
3. A：你有孩子吗？多大了？
   B：________________________________。
4. A：你家都有什么人？
   B：________________________________。
5. A：今天，您就在我这儿吃饭，怎么样？
   B：________________________________。

Dì shíliù kè
第十六课

Qù Lǔxùn Gōngyuán
去 鲁迅 公园

Language Points

a. 你明白了没有？
b. 史密斯先生一到休息天就和朋友去打高尔夫。
c. 吃了饭再看电视吧。

Text

(In the house of Mr. Jiang)

Shǐmìsī xiānsheng, nǐ qùguo Lǔxùn Gōngyuán méiyǒu?
江先生：史密斯先生，你去过鲁迅公园没有？

Méiyǒu wa. Tīngshuō gōngyuán li yǒu Lǔxùn Jìniànguǎn, shì ma?
史密斯：没有哇。听说公园里有鲁迅纪念馆，是吗？

Shì de, gōngyuán fùjìn hái yǒu Lǔxùn Gùjū ne. Wǒmen chīwán wǔfàn yīkuàir qù, zěnmeyàng?
江先生：是的，公园附近还有鲁迅故居呢。我们吃完午饭一块儿去，怎么样？

Tài hǎo le!
史密斯：太好了！

Bàba, wǒ yě qù.
文文：爸爸，我也去。

Wénwen, chīwán fàn yǐhòu shuì wǔjiào ba.
江夫人：文文，吃完饭以后睡午觉吧。

Bùma. wǒ yě qù!
文文：不嘛。我也去！

Nǐ kàn zhè háizi, yī tīng qù gōngyuán jiù bù shuì wǔjiào le.
江夫人：你看这孩子，一听去公园就不睡午觉了。

Fūrén, dài wénwen yīkuàir qù ba.
史密斯先生：夫人，带文文一块儿去吧。

Duì, yīkuàir qù ba, huílái zài shuì.
江先生：对，一块儿去吧，回来再睡。

Hǎo ba.
江 夫 人：好 吧。

Bàba、 māma、 shūshu， nǐmen zhēn hǎo!
文 文：爸爸、妈妈、叔叔，你们 真 好！

Words

1. 一…就…	yī…jiù…		as soon as
2. 再	zài	(adv.)	again
3. 听说	tīngshuō		It is said ...
4. 完	wán	(v.)	finish
5. 一块儿	yīkuàir	(adv.)	together
6. 睡	shuì	(v.)	sleep
7. 午觉	wǔjiào	(n.)	nap at noon
8. 不嘛	bùma		(children's language) no
9. 你看	nǐkàn		look
10. 孩子	háizi	(n.)	child, kid
11. 好	hǎo	(adj.)	good, nice
12. 回来	huílái		come back

Proper nouns

1. 鲁迅公园	Lǔxùn Gōngyuán
2. 鲁迅纪念馆	Lǔxùn Jìniànguǎn
3. 鲁迅故居	Lǔxùn Gùjū
4. 宋庆龄故居	Sòngqìnglíng Gùjū
5. 玉佛寺	Yùfósì

Supplementary words

1. 小笼包	xiǎolóngbāo	(n.)	bun
2. 食堂	shítáng	(n.)	dining hall, cafeteria
3. 结婚	jiéhūn	(v.)	marry

4. 留学	liúxué	(v.)	study abroad
5. 打	dǎ	(v.)	place (a telephone call)
6. 散步	sànbù	(v.)	take a walk
7. 洗澡	xǐzǎo	(v.)	take a bath
8. 时间	shíjiān	(n.)	time
9. 钱	qián	(n.)	money
10. 到	dào	(v.)	reach
11. 下班	xiàbān	(v.)	return from work

Grammatical explanation

一、"…没有?"

We have learned a kind of question with affirmation and negation combined, such as "她是不是学生?", "那个好不好?", "你去不去北京?", and "你有没有电脑?".

This type of structure can also be used to make sentences of question to ask about "completion" or "experience". Since the negation form expressing "completion" or "experience" is "没有", it must also be used in questions. For example:

(1)他找到了江先生没有? (Has he found Mr. Jiang?)

(2)你吃过上海菜没有? (Have you ever had Shanghai dishes?)

二、"一…就…"

This structure means "…一下儿,就…", "刚…就…", "如果…就…", etc, which correspond to "as soon as ..." or "if" in English. For example:

(1)一看就明白了。 (You will understand it as soon as you have a look at it.)

(2)我一见你就高兴。 (I feel pleased as soon as I see you.)

三、"再"

① again

The word "再" means repetition of action, but only used of future actions instead of past ones. For the repetition of past actions, the word "又" should be used. For example:

(1)你再来玩儿吧。 (Come over for a visit again.)
(2)明年我再回美国。 (I'll go back to USA again.)

② "do ... and do ... again"
This structure indicates the order of actions. For example:
(1)等一个小时再去吧! (Wait for a hour before going there.)
(2)作业很多,做完了再休息。(There is a lot of homework. Take a rest after finishing it.)

Exercise I

Please read aloud the following sentences.

1. ① 你去过鲁迅公园没有?
② 你的太太来过上海没有?
③ 你吃过小笼包没有?
④ 卡森先生学过汉语没有?
⑤ 他们都见过你没有?

2. ① 听说公园里有鲁迅纪念馆。
② 听说学校里有食堂。
③ 听说小王结婚了。
④ 听说他去美国留学了。
⑤ 听说他是总经理。

3. ① 我们吃完午饭一块儿去怎么样?
② 我们打完电脑一块儿去吃饭吧。
③ 我们做完作业以后去散步吧。
④ 我做完饭想休息一会儿。
⑤ 看完电视,马上洗澡。

4. ① 一听去公园就不睡午觉了。
② 一有时间就去旅游。
③ 一有钱就买东西。
④ 一到十点就想睡觉。
⑤ 一到春天就很暖和。

5. ① 回来再睡吧。
② 下班以后再去吧。
③ 打了电话再吃饭吧。
④ 学了汉语再去中国。
⑤ 去了中国再学汉语。

Exercise II

Please practice reading the following dialogues.

1. A：史密斯先生，你去过鲁迅公园没有？
B：没有哇。
① 参观过宋庆龄故居　　参观过
② 去过玉佛寺　　没去过

2. A：你看这孩子，一听去公园就不睡午觉了。
B：夫人，带文文一块儿去吧。
① 去玩儿　　② 去看电影

3. A：对，一块儿去吧，回来再睡。
B：好吧。
① 看　　② 做

Assignment I

Please translate the following sentences into Chinese and read them aloud.

1. Have you ever been to any park in China?
2. Do you go to watch Chinese movies on Sunday?
3. What do you do after you get up?
4. I always watch TV as soon as I get home.
5. As soon as holiday comes, I go out for a tour with my friends.
6. As soon as summer comes, it becomes hot in Shanghai.
7. He becomes very happy as soon as he sees his girlfriend.
8. Have some fruit after meal.

Assignment II

Please use your own background to complete the following dialogues.

1. A：你去过鲁迅公园和鲁迅故居没有？那儿怎么样？

   B：______________________________。

2. A：今年你在中国旅游过没有？去哪儿了？

   B：______________________________。

3. A：昨天，你一下班就去哪儿了？

   B：______________________________。

4. A：一到休息天你就想干什么？

   B：______________________________。

5. A：我们学习完了以后再去散步，怎么样？

   B：______________________________。

Dì shíqī kè

第十七课

Hùzhào bù jiàn le

护照 不 见 了

Language Points

a. 这不是你的信吗?
b. 快去吧。
c. 要是有时间,我就去美国旅游。
d. 我是坐地铁去的。

Text

Zāogāo! Wǒ de hùzhào bù jiàn le.
史密斯：糟糕！ 我 的 护照 不 见 了。

Zhēnde? Shàngwǔ bù shì hái zài ma?
小 周：真的？ 上午 不 是 还 在 吗？

Shì a.
史密斯：是 啊。

Nǐ qùguo nǎli le?
小 周：你 去过 哪里 了？

Xiàwǔ wǒ qù lǐngshìguǎn bàn shǒuxù, huílái jiù bù jiàn le.
史密斯：下午 我 去 领事馆 办 手续， 回来 就 不 见 了。

Nà kuài dǎ diànhuà xiàng chūrùjìng guǎnlǐchù bàoshī ba.
小 周：那 快 打 电话 向 出入境 管理处 报失 吧。

……

Xiǎo Zhōu, wǒ de hùzhào zhǎodào le!
史密斯：小 周， 我 的 护照 找到 了！

Shì zài nǎr zhǎodào de?
小 周：是 在 哪儿 找到 的？

Chūrùjìng guǎnlǐchù. Tīngshuō shì chūzūchē sījī bāng wǒ sòngdào chūrùjìng guǎnlǐchù de.
史密斯：出入境 管理处。 听说 是 出租车 司机 帮 我 送到 出入境 管理处 的。

Tài hǎo le!
小 周：太 好 了！

Yàoshi zhǎobudào, jiù máfan le. Xiànzài wǒ mǎshàng qù chūrùjìng guǎnlǐchù qǔ hùzhào.
史密斯：要是 找不到， 就 麻烦 了。现在 我 马上 去 出入境 管理处 取 护照。

小　周：Kuài qù ba! 快去吧！

Words

1. 不是…吗	bùshì…ma		Isn't it ... ?
2. 快	kuài	(adj.)	quick
3. 要是…就…	yàoshi…jiù…		If ...
4. 是…的	shì…de		pattern for affirmation
5. 护照	hùzhào	(n.)	passport
6. 见	jiàn	(v.)	see
7. 糟糕	zāogāo	(adj.)	terrible
8. 领事馆	lǐngshìguǎn	(n.)	consulate
9. 办	bàn	(v.)	go through
10. 手续	shǒuxù	(n.)	formality
11. 出入境管理处	chūrùjìng guǎnlǐchù	(n.)	the Exit & Entry Administration Office
12. 报失	bàoshī	(v.)	report the loss
13. 找	zhǎo	(v.)	look for
14. 帮	bāng	(v.)	help
15. 送	sòng	(v.)	give
16. 到	dào	(v.)	go to (some place)
17. 取	qǔ	(v.)	fetch

Supplementary words

1. 服务员	fúwùyuán	(n.)	waitor, waitress
2. 车站	chēzhàn	(n.)	station
3. 去年	qùnián	(n.)	last year
4. 开玩笑	kāiwánxiào		joke, make fun of
5. 打的	dǎdī		take a taxi
6. 跑步	pǎobù	(v.)	run
7. 比赛	bǐsài	(v., n.)	match, compete

8. 精彩	jīngcǎi	(adj.)	wonderful
9. 着急	zháojí	(adj.)	impatient
10. 慢	màn	(adj.)	slow
11. 认真	rènzhēn	(adj.)	serious
12. 热情	rèqíng	(adj.)	passionate
13. 服务	fúwù	(v.)	serve
14. 刚才	gāngcái	(n.)	just now
15. 丢	diū	(v.)	lose
16. 坏	huài	(adj.)	bad

Grammatical explanation

一、"不是…吗?" as a rhetorical question

"不是" means "isn't", as in "她不是学生" (She is not a student) and "这不是我的书" (This is not my book). "吗" indicates a question. When they are used together, the structure "不是…吗?" means "Isn't it ... ?" It is similar to a negative question in English. For example:

(1)这不是你的吗?　　(Isn't this yours?)

(2)你们不是去北京吗?　　(Is it not Beijing that you will go to?)

二、Adjective (地) + verb

In Lesson Nine, the structure "好好儿休息休息" was introduced. The auxiliary word "地" can be inserted to form "好好儿地休息休息". Similar examples are "好好儿休息", "努力工作", "慢慢吃", etc. There are several ways to supplement and explain verbs and the use of "地" is one of them. For example:

(1)大家高兴地唱歌。　　(Everybody sings happily.)

(2)认真地学习。　　(Study seriously.)

三、"向" idicating the object of an action

The word "向" can be used to indicate the direction or object of an action and it is similar to such words as "对", "和" and "跟".

(1)向前看。　　(Look ahead.)

(2)向她学习。　　(Learn from her.)

四、“是…的”

The word “是” is used to mean “is”, such as “这是书”(This is a book) and “她是我们的老师”(She is our teacher). It is normally not used together with a verb or adjective in a sentence. For instance, “我去” is acceptable while “我是去” is not; “他高兴” is acceptable while “他是高兴” is not.

However, the sentence “我是坐地铁去的” is acceptable because it is a special expression with the combination of both “是” and “的”, implying an explanation of place, time and method. It is generally used of a past action or an action which has begun.

(1)她是来学汉语的。(She came to study Chinese.)

(2)我是昨天来的。 (I came yesterday.)

五、“帮我” + verb

The word “帮” means “help”, as in “帮你” and “帮她”. In a more complex structure which means “help somebody do something”, the word order is “帮 + person + verb”.

(1)帮妹妹打扫房间。(I'll help my younger sister to clean the room.)

(2)帮朋友做作业。 (I'll help my friend to do homework.)

六、“要是…,就…”

In such instances as “我要钱” and “我要这个”, the word “要” means “want ...”.

When it is used together with a verb, as in “我要见老师” and “你要打电话吗”, it means “want to do ...” and “must do”.

In addition, it has the meaning “if” and is generally used in the form of “要是”, which can be taken as one single word and is used together with the word “就”.

(1)你要是想学习汉语,就来我们的学校吧。(Come to our school if you want to study Chinese.)

(2)要是黄老师不在,就给你打电话。 (I'll call you if Mr. Huang is absent.)

七、"送到"、"找到" and "找不到"

Here two points must be made clear. First, the word "到" has two meanings; second, the word "不" means "can't"

In the case of "送到", the word "到" is used as a preposition with the meaning of "to" or "unto", which implies the direction or completion of an action. So the expression "送到" means "deliver to".

In the case of "找到", the word "到" is used as an adverb with the meaning of the completion of an action. For instance, "买到" means "buy" and "what was bought is in hand".

With the negation word "不" inserted within "找到" and "买到", they mean that the action cannot be completed, which will be further explained in Lesson Nineteen.

(1)找不到。 (It cannot be found.)

(2)买不到。 (It cannot be bought.)

Exercise I

Please read aloud the following sentences.

1. ① 我的护照不见了。
   ② 小王的帽子不见了。
   ③ 他的孩子不见了。

2. ① 上午不是还在吗?
   ② 她不是宾馆的服务员吗?
   ③ 这里不是车站吗?
   ④ 那不是东方明珠电视塔吗?
   ⑤ 你不是在学汉语吗?

3. ① 听说是司机帮我送到出入境管理处的。
   ② 史密斯先生是去年来中国的。
   ③ 我是开玩笑的。
   ④ 她是打的来的。
   ⑤ 他是跑步来的。

4. ① 要是找不到,就麻烦了。

② 要是有时间，我就去美国旅游。
③ 要是太贵，就不买了。
④ 要是今天的比赛精彩我就看。
⑤ 要是你着急就先去吧。

5. ① 快去吧。
② 慢走。
③ 好好儿地学习吧。
④ 认真地工作。
⑤ 热情地服务。

Exercise II

Please practice reading the following dialogues.

1. A：糟糕！我的护照不见了。
B：真的？上午不是还在吗？
① 钱包　　刚才　　② 行李　　昨天

2. A：要是找不到，就麻烦了。
B：是啊！
① 钥匙丢了　　② 电脑坏了

3. A：现在我马上去出入境管理处取护照。
B：快去吧！
① 打扫房间　　打扫
② 做饭　　做

Assignment I

Please translate the following sentences into Chinese and read them aloud.

1. It's terrible! I've lost the keys of our company.
2. Ah, the television set has broken down.
3. Isn't this what you have bought?
4. Isn't this Mr. Jiang's house?

5. We have no time to lose. Let's hurry.
6. It is Sunday tomorrow. I'll take a good rest.
7. If he goes, I'll not go.
8. If I am in China, I'll learn Chinese at school everyday.

Assignment II

Please use your own background to complete the following dialogues.

1. A：你来中国以后，丢过东西没有？

   B：______________________________。

2. A：要是你丢了护照，怎么办？跟史密斯先生一样马上去报失吗？

   B：____________________________________。

3. A：要是我有很多时间就去中国旅游，你呢？

   B：______________________________。

4. A：你是坐飞机来上海的吗？

   B：______________________________。

5. A：你每天是坐地铁上班的？还是坐出租车上班的？

   B：______________________________。

Dì shíbā kè
第十八课

Zài yínháng
在 银行

Language Points

a. 我把今天的工作做完了。
b. 她不做,只好我做。
c. 这个比那个便宜。

Text

史　密　斯：Xiǎojie, wǒ fù diànhuàfèi.
小姐，我付电话费。

银行服务员：Qǐng nín bǎ diànhuàfèi zhàngdān gěi wǒ.
请您把电话费账单给我。

史　密　斯：Hǎo.
好。

银行服务员：Xiānsheng, zhè zhāng bùshì diànhuàfèi zhàngdān.
先生，这张不是电话费账单。

史　密　斯：Āiya, wǒ bǎ diànhuàfèi zhàngdān nácuò le, zhǐhǎo míngtiān zài lái le.
哎呀，我把电话费账单拿错了，只好明天再来了。

银行服务员：Shì ma? Xiānsheng, wǒmen zhèr yǒu zìdòng dàijiāo fúwù, nín shēnqǐng yǐhòu, kěyǐ bùyòng měicì lái yínháng fùfèi le.
是吗？先生，我们这儿有自动代交服务，您申请以后，可以不用每次来银行付费了。

史　密　斯：Zhēnde ma? Nà bǐ xiànzài fāngbiàn le. Hǎo, wǒ xiànzài jiù shēnqǐng ba.
真的吗？那比现在方便了。好，我现在就申请吧。

银行服务员：Nàme, qǐng nín tián yīxiàr shēnqǐngbiǎo.
那么，请您填一下儿申请表。

史　密　斯：Xièxie.
谢谢。

Words

1. 把　bǎ　(prep.)　(followed by object to put it before verb)

2. 只好	zhǐhǎo	(adv.)	have no choice but ...
3. 比	bǐ	(prep.)	than
4. 付	fù	(v.)	pay
5. 费	fèi	(n.)	fee
6. 账单	zhàngdān	(n.)	bill
7. 拿	ná	(v.)	take, bring
8. 代	dài	(n.)	do something on behalf of
9. 交	jiāo	(v.)	pay
10. 申请	shēnqǐng	(v.)	apply
11. 可以	kěyǐ	(aux.,v.)	may
12. 不用	bùyòng	(adv.)	unnecessarily
13. 每次	měicì	(n.)	every time
14. 那么	nàme	(conj.)	then
15. 填	tián	(v.)	fill in
16. 申请表	shēnqǐngbiǎo	(n.)	application form

Supplementary words

1. 号码	hàomǎ	(n.)	number
2. 单位	dānwèi	(n.)	company
3. 地址	dìzhǐ	(n.)	address
4. 记	jì	(v.)	remember
5. 餐厅	cāntīng	(n.)	restaurant
6. 颜色	yánsè	(n.)	color
7. 成绩	chéngjì	(n.)	grade
8. 难	nán	(adj.)	difficult
9. 自来水	zìláishuǐ	(n.)	tap water
10. 电	diàn	(n.)	electricity
11. 煤气	méiqì	(n.)	gas
12. 订购	dìnggòu	(v.)	order
13. 货	huò	(n.)	goods

Grammatical explanation

一、Sentence with the word“把”

In a Chinese sentence where there is a transitive verb used as the predicate, the object is normally put after the verb, such as“写信”and“付电话费”. But when the preposition“把”is used, the object will be put before the verb.

In this case, the verb cannot be used in isolation, but used with the addition of other words, such as“拿 ＋ 错”。

(1)你把本子带来了吗？ (Have you brought the notebook with you?)

(2)我把今天的工作做完了。(I've finished today's work.)

二、“…,只好…”

This structure means“... can only do ...”, with the first half indicating the reason.

(1)时间晚了,只好明天再去。
(It is late and we have no choice but to go tomorrow.)

(2)我们不知道她的电话号码,只好等她来。
(We don't know her telephone number, so we have no choice but to wait for her to come.)

三、“比”used in comparison

① “The object of comparison ＋ adjective”

This structure is used in comparison and in its negative form“不”can be used, but“没有…(那么)”is used more often. The word order of comparison is as follows:

…比 ＋ object of comparison ＋ adjective

(1)这里比那里干净。 (This place is cleaner than that one.)

(2)这个比那个好。 (This is better than that.)

② Negative form

(1)这里没有那里(那么)干净。(This place is not as clean as that one.)

(2)这个没有那个(那么)好。(This is not as good as that.)

(3)这里不比那里干净。 (This place is not cleaner than that one.)

(4)这个不比那个好。 (This is not better than that.)

四、"可以" + verb

The structure "要/想 + verb" has been introduced in the above. The word "可以" can also be followed by verbs to mean "can do", implying "possibility" and "permission". In this lesson, the word "可以" is followed by "不用" which means "don't need to do ...". Therefore, "可以不用 ..." means "It's OK that ... don't do ...", that is, "... don't need to do ...".

(1)我可以帮你打扫办公室。(I can help you clean the office.)
(2)这儿可以吃东西吗?　(Can I eat food here?)
(3)下午可以不去学校。　(We don't need to go to school in the afternoon.)

五、"不用"

The negative forms of "要/想 + verb" will be summarized in the following.

The structure "想 + verb" means "want to do". Its negative form is "不 + 想", which means "do not want to do."

The structure "要 + verb" has two meanings: "want to do ..." and "must do ...". Their negative form is not "不要", which means "prohibition", that is, "mustn't do ...".

The negative forms of "要 + verb" are as follows:

要…(want to do ...)→不想
要…(must do ...)　→不用

(1)我也知道,你不用问他。(I also know it and you don't need to ask him.)
(2)你不用付费。　(You don't need to pay.)

Exercise I

Please read aloud the following sentences.

1. ① 请您把电话费账单给我。
② 请把你的电话号码告诉我吧。
③ 请把你的单位地址写一下儿。
④ 请你把房间打扫一下儿。
⑤ 请你把衣服洗一下儿。

2. ① 我把电话费账单拿错了，只好明天再来了。
   ② 我把他的手机号码记错了，只好再问一下儿了。
   ③ 她把我的午饭吃了，只好去餐厅吃了。
   ④ 没有钱了，只好不买了。
   ⑤ 太累了，只好休息了。

3. ① 那比现在方便了。
   ② 这种颜色比那种颜色漂亮。
   ③ 她的成绩比我好。
   ④ 今天的作业比昨天难。
   ⑤ 这里比那里安静。

4. ① 那不比现在方便。
   ② 这种颜色不比那种颜色漂亮。
   ③ 她的成绩不比我好。
   ④ 今天的作业不比昨天难。
   ⑤ 这里不比那里安静。

5. ① 那没有现在方便。
   ② 这种颜色没有那种颜色漂亮。
   ③ 她的成绩没有我好。
   ④ 今天的作业没有昨天难。
   ⑤ 这里没有那里安静。

Exercise II

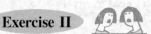

Please practice reading the following dialogues.

1. A：我把电话费账单拿错了，只好明天再来了。
   B：是吗？
   ① 自来水费和电费
   ② 煤气费

2. A：我们这儿有自动代交服务，您申请以后，可以不用每次来银行付费了。

B：真的吗？

① 订购　　商店买

② 送货　　商店买

3. A：好，我现在就申请吧。

B：那么，请您填一下儿申请表。

A：谢谢！

① 写　　这张申请表

② 付　　申请费

Assignment I

Please translate the following sentences into Chinese and read them aloud.

1. I told Mr. Zhang about this matter.
2. He wrote again the characters that he had wrongly written.
3. I want to buy a car, but since I don't have money, I have no choice but not to buy one.
4. I've got a flu and headache so that I have no choice but to take medicine.
5. Because I've been very busy today, I have no choice but to work overtime.
6. This room is bigger than that one.
7. This kind of tea is not as good as that one.
8. It is not as cold in Shanghai as in Beijing.

Assignment II

Please use your own background to complete the following dialogues.

1. A：你去过中国的银行没有？

   B：______________________________。

2. A：你每月去银行付电话费吗？

   B：______________________________。

3. A：你知道中国的银行也有自动付款服务吗？

B：________________________________。

4. A：你每月的电话费多少钱？

B：________________________________。

5. A：我觉得中国的银行很方便。你呢？

B：________________________________。

Dì shíjiǔ kè

第十九课

Jiābān

加班

Language Points

a. 这几天我累得很。

b. 这些工作,你一个人做得完吗?

c. 这个便宜,那个贵得多。

Text

Shǐmìsī xiānsheng, gāngcái Kǎsēn xiānsheng lái
秘　书：史密斯　先生，　刚才　卡森　先生　来
diànhuà, shuō yuē nín jīnwǎn yīqǐ chī fàn. Qǐng
电话，　说　约　您　今晚　一起　吃　饭。请
nín gěi tā huí gè diànhuà.
您　给　他　回　个　电话。

Jīnwǎn? Bù xíng a.
史密斯：今晚？　不　行　啊。

Zěnme le?
秘　书：怎么　了？

Jīntiān wǒ mángdehěn, wǎnshang yěxǔ yào
史密斯：今天　我　忙得很，　晚上　也许　要
jiābān le.
加班　了。

Shì ma?
秘　书：是　吗？

Xiàwǔ kāiwán huì yǐhòu, háiyào xiě liǎngfèn
史密斯：下午　开完　会　以后，　还要　写　两份
bàogào ne.
报告　呢。

Jīntiān xiědewán ma?
秘　书：今天　写得完　吗？

Dàgài xiědewán ba.
史密斯：大概　写得完　吧。

Nà nín xiěwán yǐhòu, wǒ mǎshàng dǎ zì.
秘　书：那　您　写完　以后，我　马上　打　字。

Hǎo, nàyàng huì kuàideduō.
史密斯：好，　那样　会　快得多。

Nà Kǎsēn xiānsheng nàr zěnme bàn?
秘　书：那　卡森　先生　那儿　怎么　办？

Wǒ lái dǎ diànhuà.
史密斯：我 来 打 电话。

Words

1.	几	jǐ	(pron.)	how many
2.	…得很	…dehěn		(used after adjectives and some adverbs) indicating high extent
3.	得	de	(aux.)	(used after verbs)
4.	…得多	…deduō		(in comparison) much
5.	加班	jiābān		work overtime
6.	来	lái	(v.)	(used before another verb indicating future)
7.	约	yuē	(v.)	invite, make an appointment
8.	回	huí	(v.)	return, reply
9.	行	xíng	(adj., v.)	(used in reply) OK
10.	怎么	zěnme	(pron.)	how (asking about situation, manner, etc.)
11.	也许	yěxǔ	(adv.)	maybe
12.	开	kāi	(v.)	hold (a meeting), attend (a meeting)
13.	会/会议	huì/huìyì	(n.)	meeting
14.	份	fèn	(cl.)	(of newspaper, file, etc.)
15.	报告	bàogào	(n.)	report
16.	大概…吧	dàgài…ba		probably, assumably
17.	打	dǎ	(v.)	typewrite
18.	好	hǎo	(n.)	(expressing agreement) OK, all right
19.	那样	nàyàng	(pron.)	that way
20.	会	huì	(aux., v.)	(expressing possibility)

Supplementary words

1. 留言	liúyán	(v.)	leave a word
2. 首	shǒu	(cl.)	(used of poems)
3. 歌	gē	(n.)	song
4. 董事长	dǒngshìzhǎng	(n.)	chairman of the board
5. 自行车	zìxíngchē	(n.)	bicycle
6. 来得及	láidejí		there's still time
7. 声音	shēngyīn	(n.)	sound
8. 辛苦	xīnkǔ	(adj.)	hard, painstaking
9. 人口	rénkǒu	(n.)	population
10. 闲	xián	(adj.)	unoccupied, free
11. 早	zǎo	(adj.)	early
12. 早饭	zǎofàn	(n.)	breakfast

Grammatical explanation

一、Adjective ＋"得很"

The structure "得很" is used after adjectives to mean "to a high extent" or "of high degree".

(1)快得很。 (Very fast.)

(2)精彩得很。 (Very wonderful.)

二、"也许…" and "大概…吧"

The two structures express a mood of speculation on the part of the speaker, but they are a little different. The structure "也许…" means "possibility without certainty"; the structure "大概…吧" implies "probability".

(1)他们也许不在家。 (Perhaps they are not in.)

(2)他今天大概要加班吧。(Today he'll probably work overtime.)

三、Verb ＋ "得…"

In such a structure, "得…" means "possibility" or "capability". In the negative form "得…" will be changed into "不…".

(1)你明天回得来吗？我明天回不来。

(Can you come back tomorrow? I can't come back tomorrow.)

(2)今天的作业你做得完吗？做不完。

(Can you finish today's homework? I can't.)

四、Adjective ＋“得多”

This structure is the same as “得很”, but it is used in comparison

(1)那儿暖和，这儿冷得多。

(It is warm there while it is much colder here.)

(2)她的孩子可爱得多。(Her kid is much more lovely.)

Exercise I

Please read aloud the following sentences.

1. ① 请您给他回个电话。
   ② 请您给我打个电话。
   ③ 请您给我留个言。
   ④ 请你给我们唱首歌。
   ⑤ 请你给她打扫一下儿房间。

2. ① 今天我忙得很。
   ② 这几天我累得很。
   ③ 昨天他高兴得很。
   ④ 这儿的东西便宜得很。
   ⑤ 汉语难得很。

3. ① 晚上也许要加班了。
   ② 明天也许要开会。
   ③ 也许她不懂。
   ④ 我也许明年去美国。
   ⑤ 他也许是董事长。

4. ① 大概写得完吧。
   ② 大概这是他的自行车吧。
   ③ 大概上海的夏天很热吧。

④ 大概他在洗澡吧。
⑤ 大概时间来得及吧。

5. ① 今天写得完吗？
② 这封英文信你看得懂吗？
③ 这些作业下午做得完吗？
④ 我的声音你听得见吗？
⑤ 明天的机票买得到吗？

6. ① 今天写不完。
② 这封英文信我看不懂。
③ 这些作业下午做不完。
④ 你的声音我听不见。
⑤ 明天的机票买得到。

7. ① 那样会快得多。
② 昨天暖和，今天冷得多。
③ 他的工作很忙，比我辛苦得多。
④ 王小姐比以前漂亮得多。
⑤ 上海的人口比旧金山多得多。

Exercise II

Please practice reading the following dialogues.

1. A：今天我忙得很，晚上也许要加班。
B：是吗？
① 闲　　去看电影
② 累　　早睡觉

2. A：今天写得完吗？
B：大概写得完吧。
① 干得完　　干不完
② 买得到　　买得到

3. A：那您写完以后，我马上打字。
   B：好，这样可以快得多。
   ① 吃　　　洗碗
   ② 起床　　做早饭

Assignment I

Please translate the following sentences into Chinese and read them aloud.

1. There are a lot of shops near my house, so that place is hilarious.
2. Fruits are very cheap here in summer.
3. Can you finish this report tomorrow?
4. Can you understand newspapers in Chinese?
5. She is much busier than I.
6. This piece of clothes is much more beautiful than that one.
7. This is perhaps Mr. Smith's.
8. It may rain tomorrow.

Assignment II

Please use your own background to complete the following dialogues.

1. A：你每个月都加班吗？
   B：______________________________。

2. A：你经常一个人加班，还是和公司的人一起加班？
   B：______________________________。

3. A：你经常写报告吗？
   B：______________________________。

4. A：你会写汉语报告吗？
   B：______________________________。

5. A：我的美国朋友比中国朋友多得多，你呢？

B：________________________________。

Dì èrshí kè

第二十课

Fā diànzǐyóujiàn

发 电子邮件

Language Points

a. 他先来上海,然后去北京。
b. 我的手机被/叫/让人偷了。
c. 这是从美国买来的。
d. 今晚我有事,不能去音乐会了。

Text

	Shǐmìsī xiānsheng, tīngshuō zuówǎn nǐ jiābān le,
江先生：	史密斯 先生， 听说 昨晚 你 加班 了，
	shì ma?
	是 吗？
	Shì de, jì gěi Huáshèngdùn zǒnggōngsī de liǎng fèn
史密斯：	是 的， 寄 给 华盛顿 总公司 的 两 份
	bàogào dōu xiěwán le.
	报告 都 写完 了。
	Xīnkǔ le.
江先生：	辛苦 了。
	Xiànzài wǒ xiǎng xiān dǎyìn yīxiàr, ránhòu
史密斯：	现在 我 想 先 打印 一下儿， 然后
	mǎshàng fā chuánzhēn gěi Huáshèngdùn.
	马上 发 传真 给 华盛顿。
	Shǐmìsī xiānsheng, dǎyìnzhǐ gāng bèi yòngwán, wǒ
秘　书：	史密斯 先生， 打印纸 刚 被 用完， 我
	qù nálái.
	去 拿来。
	Háishi fā diànzǐyóujiàn kuài ba.
江先生：	还是 发 电子邮件 快 吧。
	Shì a. Kěshì, zhè jǐ tiān wǒ de diànnǎo bù
史密斯：	是 啊。 可是， 这 几 天 我 的 电脑 不
	tài zhèngcháng, bù néng fā yóujiàn le.
	太 正常， 不 能 发 邮件 了。
	Nà yòng wǒ de diànnǎo ba.
江先生：	那 用 我 的 电脑 吧。
	Xièxie.
史密斯：	谢谢。
	Shǐmìsī xiānsheng, tā de diànnǎo wǒ yě hěn
秘　书：	史密斯 先生， 他 的 电脑 我 也 很
	shúxī, wǒ lái fā ba.
	熟悉，我 来 发 吧。

Bàituō le.
史密斯： 拜托 了。

Words

1. 先…然后…	xiān…ránhòu…		First . . . and then
2. 被/叫/让	bèi/jiào/ràng	(prep.)	(used in passive voice) by
3. 偷	tōu	(v.)	steal
4. 从	cóng	(prep.)	(indicating the starting point) from
5. 能	néng	(aux. v.)	(expressing ability) can
6. 发	fā	(v.)	send (email, fax)
7. 电子邮件	diànzǐyóujiàn	(n.)	email
8. 昨晚	zuówǎn	(n.)	last night, yesterday evening.
9. 辛苦了	xīnkǔle		Thanks for your hard work!
10. 打印	dǎyìn	(v.)	print
11. 传真	chuánzhēn	(n.)	fax
12. 纸	zhǐ	(n.)	paper
13. 刚	gāng	(adv.)	just now
14. 用	yòng	(v.)	use
15. 可是	kěshì	(conj.)	but
16. 熟悉	shúxī	(v.)	be familiar with (to)
17. 拜托	bàituō	(v.)	please
18. 正常	zhèngcháng	(adj.)	in good order

Supplementary words

1. 计划	jìhuà	(v.,n.)	plan
2. 搞	gǎo	(v.)	do
3. 收拾	shōushi	(v.)	tidy up, do out

4. 生词	shēngcí	(n.)	new words
5. 听写	tīngxiě	(v.,n.)	dictate
6. 练习	liànxí	(v.,n.)	exercise
7. 名字	míngzi	(n.)	name
8. 饮料	yǐnliào	(n.)	drink
9. 搬	bān	(v.)	move
10. 快递	kuàidì	(n.)	express delivery
11. 带	dài	(v.)	bring, carry
12. 上课	shàngkè	(v.)	have classes
13. 来不及	láibují		it's too late
14. 好	hǎo	(adj.)	healthy
15. 坏	huài	(adj.)	bad

Grammatical explanation

一、Verb ＋ "给"

Here the usage of "给" will be summed up. As an ordinary verb, it means "to give somebody something" and "to give something to somebody" (Lesson Nine and Lesson Eighteen), such as "给你" and "给你这个".

In addition, it can also be used to indicate the object of an action. The word order is "给 ＋ person/thing ＋ verb", which means "to do something for a person/thing", such as "给你买东西" (to buy something for you) and "给他打电话" (to make a phone call to you).

What needs to be noticed is that the word order of "给 ＋ person/thing ＋ verb" can also be changed into the form "verb ＋ 给".

(1)请把这本书借给我。 (Please lend this book to me.)

(2)那张传真我已经发给你了。(I've sent the fax to you.)

二、"先…然后…"

This structure idicates the order of actions. For instance,

(1)你先睡觉,然后去工作吧。

(Take a sleep first and then go to work.)

(2)我先休息,然后吃饭。

(I'll take a rest first and then have my meal.)

三、Passive voice with “被/叫/让”

In Chinese the word order for passive voice is “被/叫/让 + person + verb ...”.

(1)我的自行车被他骑去了。
(My bicycle has been taken for use by him.)

(2)你的电脑被谁弄坏了?(By whom was your computer spoiled?)

四、Verb + “来/去”

The two words “来” and “去” have a lot of usages.

① Ordinary verbs

(1)他来了。 (He has come.)

(2)我去北京。 (I'll go to Beijing.)

② Meaning “actively” or “voluntarily” (only used of “来”)

(1)我来试一试。 (Let me have a try.)

(2)我来看一看。 (Let me have a look.)

③ Indicating direction

(1)拿来。 (Bring it here.)

(2)拿去。 (Take it away.)

五、“能” + verb

This structure is the same as “要”, “想”, “会” and “可以” which have been learned previously. All of them can be used to express “possibility”.

(1)你能用电脑打字吗? (Can you type with a computer?)

(2)现在能申请吗? (Can I apply now?)

Exercise I

Please read aloud the following sentences.

1. ① 我想先打印一下儿,然后马上发传真给华盛顿。
② 他先来上海,然后去北京。
③ 我们先计划一下儿,然后一起搞吧。
④ 星期天,我先收拾房间,然后去超市买东西。

⑤ 请你先记生词，然后做听写练习。

2. ① 打印纸刚被用完。
② 我的手机被人偷了。
③ 我的名字让他搞错了。
④ 自行车叫我丢了。
⑤ 饮料都让他们喝完了。

3. ① 打印纸刚被用完，我去拿来。
② 这是从美国买来的。
③ 桌子和椅子都搬来了。
④ 快递公司送来了我的邮件。
⑤ 她给朋友带来礼物了。

4. ① 他的书小周拿去了。
② 小王休息去了。
③ 史密斯先生回去了。
④ 我的妹妹留学去了。
⑤ 她上课去了。

5. ① 这几天我的电脑不太正常，不能发邮件了。
② 今晚我有事，不能去听音乐会了。
③ 时间来不及了，我们不能去了。
④ 感冒好了，我能上班了。
⑤ 史密斯先生能说中文和英文。

Exercise II

Please practice reading the following dialogues.

1. A：林达，明天是休息天了，你打算怎么过？
B：我想上午先洗衣服，然后去超市买东西。下午去见一个朋友。
① 打扫房间　　做饭
② 去美容店　　去饭店吃饭

2. A：打印纸刚被用完，我去拿来。
   B：谢谢！
   ① 红茶　喝　买
   ② 杯子　用　取

3. A：这几天我的电脑不太正常，不能发邮件了。
   B：那用我的电脑吧。
   ① 不好　用
   ② 坏了　打

Assignment I

Please translate the following sentences into Chinese and read them aloud.

1. After getting up in the morning, I have breakfast while watching TV, and then go to my company.
2. After getting home every afternoon, she has some dim sum before she does her homework.
3. The tea has been used up.
4. The cake has been eaten up by her.
5. I bought and took back a lot of books yesterday.
6. The dictionary has been taken away by him.
7. I have caught a cold and cannot go to school tomorrow.
8. My watch has broken down.

Assignment II

Please use your own background to complete the following dialogues.

1. A：你每天发电子邮件吗？

   B：______________________________。

2. A：你去旅游时，笔记本电脑也想带去吗？

   B：______________________________。

3. A：你被人偷过东西吗？

B：＿＿＿＿＿＿＿＿＿＿＿＿＿＿＿＿＿＿＿＿。

4. A：你的手机是从哪儿买来的？

B：＿＿＿＿＿＿＿＿＿＿＿＿＿＿＿＿＿＿＿＿。

5. A：我每天回家以后，先洗澡，然后吃饭、看电视。你呢？

B：＿＿＿＿＿＿＿＿＿＿＿＿＿＿＿＿＿＿＿＿＿＿＿＿＿。

English translations of texts

Lesson One I'm an American living abroad

Text

Mr. Smith: Hello! I'm Smith and I'm an American living abroad.
Miss Wang: Hello! My name is Wang and his name is Jiang.
Mr. Smith: Hello, Mr. Jiang.
Mr. Jiang: Hello, Mr. Smith.
Miss Wang: Sit down, please.
Mr. Smith: Thanks!

Lesson Two This is your key.

Text

Mr. Smith: Would you please tell me who the administrator is?
Apartment administrator: I am the administrator.
Mr. Smith: I am Smith from the American software company.
Apartment administrator: You are Mr. Smith? Hello!
Mr. Smith: Hello!
Apartment administrator: Your room is Room 48 in Building 11. This is the key to your room.
Mr. Smith: Thanks!

Lesson Three The office in on the second floor.

Text

Miss Wang: This is the office. The inquiry office and the reception room are on the first floor.
Mr. Smith: Is the office also on the first floor?
Miss Wang: No, the office is not on the first floor, but on the second floor.
Mr. Smith: Where is your office?
Miss Wang: My office is on the second floor, to the left of the elevator.
Mr. Smith: Which floor is the meeting room on?
Miss Wang: The meeting room is also on the second floor, opposite the elevator.
Mr. Smith: I see.

Lesson Four There are some guests in the reception room.

Text

Mr. Smith: Miss, are there any people in the reception room?

Inquiry office: Yes, there are. They are Mr. Jiang and three guests from the parent company.

Mr. Smith: Then are there any people in the meeting room upstairs?

Inquiry office: Meeting room? Wait a moment please... Mr. Smith, there is no one in the meeting room.

Mr. Smith: Really? Thanks!

Lesson Five A Holiday

Text

Secretary: Mr. Smith, it is Saturday tomorrow. How will you spend the holiday?

Mr. Smith: What do you mean? I cannot understand what you said.

Secretary: What will you do on Saturday and Sunday?

Mr. Smith: Oh, I'll play golf on Saturday. I'll wash my clothes on Sunday morning and learn Chinese at one o'clock. What about you?

Secretary: I'll stay at home on Saturday and go to watch a movie on Sunday.

Lesson Six Going to the supermarket

Text

Xiao Zhou: Mr. Smith!

Mr. Smith: Xiao Zhou!

Xiao Zhou: Where are you going?

Mr. Smith: I'm going to the supermarket to do some shopping.

Xiao Zhou: Really? So am I.

Mr. Smith: What are you going to buy?

Xiao Zhou: I'm going to buy some batteries. And you?

Mr. Smith: I'm going to buy some fruit.

(Entering the supermarket)

Xiao Zhou: Batteries are over there. Let's go there first.

Mr. Smith: OK. I'll buy some tapes along the way.

Lesson Seven Seeing a friend

Text

(The apartment doorman is calling Mr. Smith.)

Apartment doorkeeper:	Hello, I'd like to speak to Mr. Smith in Room 48.
Mr. Smith:	This is Mr. Smith. Who is that...?
Apartment doorkeeper:	This is the doorkeeper. You are wanted downstairs.
Mr. Smith:	Thanks! I'm coming downstairs right now.

(In the lobby of the apartment)

Mr. and Mrs. Brown:	Mr. Smith, it has been a long time since we met!
Mr. Smith:	A long time! I have been waiting for you.
Mr. Brown:	Really? We first went to the hotel and left our luggage there.
Mr. Smith:	Is this the first time for Mrs. Brown to come to China?
Mrs. Brown:	Yes.
Mr. Smith:	I'm free tomorrow. What about going with me to Pudong for a visit?
Mr. and Mrs. Brown:	Thanks!

Lesson Eight Visiting the Oriental Pearl TV Tower

Text

(In a taxi)

Mr. Smith:	(To the driver) Is that a tunnel ahead?
Taxi Driver:	Yes, after passing through the tunnel we'll reach Pudong.
Mr. Smith:	This is Pudong.
Mrs. Brown:	The Roads in Pudong are really wide.
Mr. Brown:	The Buildings here are both tall and wonderful.
Mr. Smith:	Look, there is the Oriental Pearl TV Tower.
Mr. and Mrs. Brown:	So high!
Taxi Driver:	This is the Oriental Pearl TV Tower. Folks, please remember to take your things with you.
Mr. Smith: Mr. and Mrs. Brown:	Thanks!

Lesson Nine He's caught a cold.

Text

Secretary: Mr. Smith, what's the matter with you?
Smith: I've got a headache and a cough.
Secretary: Have you been to the doctor?
Smith: Yes, I have. The doctor said I caught a cold, so he prescribed for me some granules for influenza.
Secretary: Do you know how to take them?
Smith: Yes. Since granules have fewer side effects, I like this kind of Chinese medicine.
Secretary: Really? But you still need to have a good rest after taking the medicine.
Smith: I see.

Lesson Ten Birthday

Text

(After work)
Xiao Zhang: Mr. Smith, this is the first time you have had a birthday since you came to Shanghai, isn't it?
Smith: Yes.
Colleagues: Happy birthday!
Smith: Thank you!
Mr. Jiang: Mr. Smith, this is a birthday cake for you from all of us.
Smith: Such a big cake! At home in the USA when I have a birthday, my wife gives me a cake. Today all of you give me a cake. I feel at home and very happy.
Mr. Jiang: That is very nice!
Miss Wang: I suggest we sing Happy Birthday, then Mr. Smith can blow out the candles and cut the cake.
Colleagues: OK.

Lesson Eleven I'm looking for stamps.

Text

(In the office)
Secretary: Mr. Smith, what are you looking for?
Smith: I'm looking for stamps.

Secretary: I have some. Some are eighty fen and some sixty. Which do you want?
Smith: I want two sixty fen. But I also want a five yuan and forty fen stamp. Do you have this kind of stamp?
Secretary: No. You want to send mail to the USA, don't you?
Smith: Yes.
Secretary: Then I'll go to the post office to buy one for you.
Smith: Thanks!

Lesson Twelve At school

Text

Smith: Mr. Huang, it is a long time since we last met!
Mr. Huang: It has been a long time, Mr. Smith!
Smith: Mr. Huang, I was very busy with work last month. I'm sorry that I was absent so many times.
Mr. Huang: It's OK since you were busy. When you are not busy, lose no time to learn.
Smith: I see. I've finished my last homework, sir.
Mr. Huang: Really? Then let me have a look at your homework first.
Smith: OK.
...
Mr. Huang: Mr. Smith, you made a mistake in writing the character "包" in the word "面包" What you wrote is the Japanese character "包".
Smith: Well, yes! I'll write it again.
Mr. Huang: The other things are done properly.
Smith: Thanks!
Mr. Huang: Next, let's go to Lesson Fifteen ...

Lesson Thirteen Celebrating a festival

Text

Smith: It is International Labour Day today. There are really a lot of people on the streets!
Mr. Carsen: Yes, where shall we go for a visit?
Mrs. Carsen: Shall we take a stroll on West Nanjing Road or go to see a movie?

Mr. Jiang: It's better to watch a movie.

Smith: That's nice! I haven't seen a movie since I came to Shanghai.

Mrs. Carsen: Really? My husband and I have gone twice.

Smith: Really? It's better to go with a wife!

Mr. Jiang: Let's go to the cinema now. After watching the movie, how about having dinner together?

Smith: Wonderful! Today is a festival. Let's have some wine tonight.

Mr. and Mrs. Carsen: All right!

Lesson Fourteen Taking subway to have dinner

Text

(Coming out of the cinema)

Mrs. Carsen: What an interesting movie today!

Mr. Carsen: Er. (Turning to Smith) Smith, did you understand everything?

Smith: No! I just understood a little. I asked Mr. Jiang questions while I was watching the movie. (Turning to Mr. Jiang) Mr. Jiang, I'm really sorry to have disturbed you when we watched the movie.

Mr. Jiang: It doesn't matter. Now let's take subway Line No. 1 to go to Xujiahui to have dinner.

Smith:
Mr. and Mrs. Carsen: OK!

(Arriving at the subway station)

Mr. Jiang: I have a traffic card. And you?

Mr. and Mrs. Carsen: We also have cards.

Smith: I don't have one. So I have to go to the automatic ticket machine to buy a ticket. Please wait for me for a moment.

Mr. Jiang:
Mr. and Mrs. Carsen: OK!

Lesson Fifteen Being a guest

Text

(In the house of Mr. Jiang)

Mr. Jiang:	Mr. Smith, let me introduce you. This is my father and this is my mother.
Mr. Jiang's parents:	Hello! Welcome!
Smith:	Hello, uncle and aunt!
Wenwen:	Uncle, are you an American?
Mr. Jiang:	This is my daughter. (Turning to his daughter) Wenwen, you must first say "Hello, uncle!"
Wenwen:	Hello, uncle!
Smith:	Hello! How old are you?
Wenwen:	I'm eight.
Smith:	Come, this is a small gift for you.
Wenwen:	Thank you, uncle!
Smith:	Wenwen is really lovely!
Mrs. Jiang:	Mr. Smith, please have some tea.
Smith:	Thanks, Mrs. Jiang.
Mrs. Jiang:	Mr. Smith, will you have lunch here with us?
Smith:	Thanks! I hope I wouldn't trouble you!

Lesson Sixteen Going to Lunxun Park

Text

(In the house of Mr. Jiang)

Mr. Jiang:	Mr. Smith, have you been to Luxun Park?
Mr. Smith:	Not yet. It is said there is a memorial hall for Luxun in the park, isn't there?
Mr. Jiang:	Yes, not far from the park there is also the former residence of Luxun. After lunch shall we go there together?
Mr. Smith:	Wonderful!
Wenwen:	Can I go with you, dad?
Mrs. Jiang:	Well, it's time for you to take a nap at noon.
Wenwen:	No, I want to go there too.
Mrs. Jiang:	Look, she won't take a nap at noon as soon as she thinks about going to the park.
Mr. Smith:	Just bring Wenwen with us.

Mr. Jiang: Yes, let's go together. She can take a nap when we come back.

Mrs. Jiang: All right。

Wenwen: How kind you are, dad, mom and uncle.

Lesson Seventeen The passport is missing.

Text

Smith: It's terrible! I can't find my passport.

Xiao Zhou: Really? It was there in the morning, wasn't it?

Smith: Yes.

Xiao Zhou: Where did you go?

Smith: I went to the consulate to go through the formalities in the afternoon. It disappeared after I came back.

Xiao Zhou: Then call the Exit & Entry Administration Office quickly to report the loss.

...

Smith: Xiao Zhou, I've found my passport.

Xiao Zhou: Where did you find it?

Smith: At the Exit & Entry Administration Office. I was told that a taxi driver gave it to the office.

Xiao Zhou: Great!

Smith: I would be in trouble if it wasn't found. Now I'll go to the Administration Office at once to get it back.

Xiao Zhou: Be quick!

Lesson Eighteen In a bank

Text

Smith: I'd like to pay the fee for my telephone call service, Miss.

Bank clerk: Please give me your telephone bill.

Smith: OK. Here you are.

Bank clerk: But this is not the telephone bill, Sir.

Smith: Oops, I took the wrong bill by mistake. I'll come again tomorrow.

Bank clerk: Oh? We have an automatic collection service. After applying, you won't need to come to the bank every time to pay the fee.

Smith: Really? That would be much more convenient. OK. I'll apply now.

Bank clerk: Then fill in this application form, please.

Smith: Thanks.

Lesson Nineteen Working an extra shift

Text

Secretary:	Mr. Smith, Mr. Carsen called just now to invite you to have dinner together tonight. He asked you to call back.
Smith:	Tonight? It's inconvenient for me.
Secretary:	What's up?
Smith:	Today I have been very busy. Perhaps I'll have to work overtime.
Secretary:	Really?
Smith:	After meeting this afternoon, I have two reports to write.
Secretary:	Is it possible for you to finish writing them today?
Smith:	Perhaps it is possible.
Secretary:	After you finish, I'll type them at once.
Smith:	OK, that would be much faster.
Secretary:	Then what shall I do about Mr. Carsen?
Smith:	I'll call him.

Lesson Twenty Sending email

Text

Mr. Jiang:	Mr. Smith, I heard you had been working overtime, is that so?
Smith:	Yes, The two reports to be sent to the Washington-based parent company are finished.
Mr. Jiang:	Thank you for your hard work!
Smith:	Now I want to have them printed, then fax them to Washington right away.
Secretary:	Mr. Smith, the printer paper has just been used up. I'll fetch some.
Mr. Jiang:	Nevertheless it may be faster to send them by email.
Smith:	Yes. But my computer has not been in good order these days and it cannot be used to send email.
Mr. Jiang:	Then use my computer.
Smith:	Thanks.
Secretary:	Mr. Smith, I'm familiar with his computer. Let me send the reports.
Smith:	Please do.

Grammatical items of each lesson

Lesson one

(1)“是”and the form of its negation
(2) Interrogative sentence and “吗”
(3) The distinction between “姓”and“叫”
(4)“先生”

Lesson two

(1) Demonstrative pronouns and their plural forms
(2)“这是”and“这个是”
(3)“也”
(4)“的”
(5)“就 + 是”
(6)“是不是”as a structure for question

Lesson three

(1) The Chinese character “在” indicating places
(2) The Chinese word “不” for negation
(3)“和”
(4)“了”

Lesson four

(1)“有” indicating existence or possession
(2)“没有” as the negative form of “有”
(3)“有没有” as a question form
(4) classifier for counting things
(5)“请…”
(6)“…一下”

Lesson five

(1) Subject + verb + object
(2) Ways of expressing time
(3) Interrogative words “什么” and“怎么”
(4) Nouns + “呢”

Lesson six

(1)“去” + place
(2) To go to a palce to do something
(3)“和”
(4)“哇”

Lesson seven

(1)“了”as the auxiliary word of mood at the end of sentence
(2)“了” indicating completion
(3)“在” + nouns of place + verb
(4)“(正)在” + verb + object (+ 呢)
(5)“…,怎么样?”
(6)“是啊”

Lesson eight

(1) Adverbs such as“很”,“非常”and“真” + adjectives
(2)“热不热”

(3)“又…又…”
(4)“你们看,…”
(5) Antonyms of common adjectives
(6) Expressions of season

Lesson nine
(1)“因此”、“因为…所以…”
(2)“怎么了”
(3) Repetition of verbs:“休息休息”
(4)“要”
(5)“会” with the meaning of “abiilty”

Lesson ten
(1)“跟/和/同…一样”
(2)“这么/那么…”
(3)“太…了”

Lesson eleven
(1)“要” + noun
(2)“要” + verb and “想” + verb
(3)“我要六毛的,…”in“的”
(4) The ways of expressing the concepts of money

Lesson twelve
(1)“Verb” or “verb + object” used as subject
(2) Subject with“的”
(3)“Subject + predicate” used as subject
(4)“Adjectives” used as subject
(5) verb + “好”

Lesson thirteen
(1) Verb + “过”
(2)“…好呢?”
(3)“还是”
(4) The distinction between “两” and “二”

Lesson fourteen
(1)“都…了”
(2)“一边…一边…”
(3)“得 + verb”
(4)“…一下儿”
(5)“去” + noun + “那儿” + verb (verb + object)

Lesson fifteen
(1)“来” + verb
(2) Queations with the adverb “多”
(3)“…极了”
(4) Words addressing family members

Lesson sixteen
(1)“…没有?”
(2)“一…就…”
(3)“再”

Lesson seventeen
(1)“不是…吗?”as a rhetorical question
(2) Adjective(地) + verb
(3)“向”idicating the object of an action
(4)“是…的”
(5)“帮我” + verb

(6)“要是…,就…”
(7)“送到”、“找到”、“找不到”

Lesson eighteen
(1) Sentence with the word“把”
(2)“…,只好…”
(3)“比” used in comparison
(4)“可以” + verb
(5)“不用”

Lesson nineteen
(1) Adjective + “得很”
(2)“也许…”、“大概…吧”
(3) verb + “得…”
(4) Adjective + “得多”

Lesson twenty
(1) verb + “给”
(2)“先…然后…”
(3) Passive voice with“被/叫/让”
(4) Verb + “来/去”
(5)“能” + verb

Word list

A

1.	啊	a	(7)
2.	哎呀	āiyā	(12)
3.	安静	ānjìng	(12)

B

1.	巴士	bāshì	(9)
2.	把	bǎ	(2,18)
3.	爸爸	bàba	(15)
4.	吧	ba	(12)
5.	拜托	bàituō	(20)
6.	搬	bān	(14,20)
7.	半	bàn	(5)
8.	办	bàn	(17)
9.	办法	bànfǎ	(12)
10.	办公室	bàngōngshì	(3)
11.	办事员	bànshìyuán	(1)
12.	帮	bāng	(17)
13.	包	bāo	(6)
14.	报告	bàogào	(19)
15.	报失	bàoshī	(17)
16.	报纸	bàozhǐ	(4)
17.	杯	bēi	(11)
18.	杯子	bēizi	(4)
19.	被	bèi	(20)
20.	本	běn	(2)
21.	本子	běnzi	(2)
22.	比	bǐ	(18)
23.	笔记本	bǐjìběn	(11)
24.	比赛	bǐsài	(17)
25.	便饭	biànfàn	(15)
26.	便利店	biànlìdiàn	(3)
27.	遍	biàn	(12)
28.	宾馆	bīnguǎn	(7)
29.	饼干	bǐnggān	(6)
30.	病	bìng	(9)
31.	病人	bìngrén	(4)
32.	伯父/伯伯	bófù/bóbo	(15)
33.	伯母	bómǔ	(15)
34.	不	bù	(1)
35.	不过	bùguò	(9)
36.	不好意思	bùhǎoyìsi	(15)
37.	布朗	Bùlǎng	(2)
38.	不嘛	bùma	(16)
39.	不是…吗	bùshì…ma	(17)
40.	不要	bùyào	(8)
41.	不用	bùyòng	(18)
42.	步行街	bùxíngjiē	(6)
43.	部	bù	(2)

C

1.	菜	cài	(7)
2.	参观	cānguān	(8)
3.	餐厅	cāntīng	(18)
4.	茶	chá	(4)
5.	差	chà	(5)
6.	长	cháng	(15)
7.	唱	chàng	(10)
8.	超市	chāoshì	(6)
9.	车站	chēzhàn	(17)
10.	衬衫	chènshān	(14)
11.	成绩	chéngjì	(18)
12.	橙汁	chéngzhī	(13)
13.	吃	chī	(9)
14.	冲剂	chōngjì	(9)
15.	重	chóng	(12)
16.	出差	chūchāi	(14)
17.	出入境管理处	chūrùjìng guǎnlǐchù	(17)
18.	出租车	chūzūchē	(14)

19. 传真 chuánzhēn (20)
20. 窗口 chuāngkǒu (14)
21. 吹 chuī (10)
22. 词典 cídiǎn (2)
23. 磁带 cídài (5)
24. 次 cì (7)
25. 从 cóng (20)
26. 错 cuò (12)

D

1. 打 dǎ (5,16,19)
2. 打的 dǎdī (17)
3. 打扰 dǎrǎo (14)
4. 打扫 dǎsǎo (5)
5. 打印 dǎyìn (20)
6. 大 dà (10)
7. 大概…吧 dàgài…ba (19)
8. 大家 dàjiā (10)
9. 大连 Dàlián (13)
10. 大厦 dàshà (8)
11. 代 dài (18)
12. 带 dài (7,20)
13. 单位 dānwèi (18)
14. 蛋糕 dàngāo (10)
15. 到 dào (8,16,17)
16. 的 de (2)
17. 得 de (19)
18. …得多 deduō (19)
19. …得很 dehěn (19)
20. 得 děi (14)
21. 等 děng (4)
22. 地方 dìfang (6)
23. 地铁 dìtiě (14)
24. 地铁站 dìtiězhàn (6)
25. 地址 dìzhǐ (18)
26. 弟弟 dìdi (15)
27. 第 dì (7)
28. DVD (14)
29. 点 diǎn (5)
30. 点心 diǎnxīn (13)
31. 电 diàn (18)
32. 电池 diànchí (6)
33. 电话 diànhuà (7)
34. 电话卡 diànhuàkǎ (2)
35. 电脑 diànnǎo (3)
36. 电视 diànshì (6)
37. 电梯 diàntī (3)
38. 电影 diànyǐng (5)
39. 电影院 diànyǐngyuàn (13)
40. 电子邮件 diànzǐyóujiàn (20)
41. 订购 dìnggòu (18)
42. 丢 diū (17)
43. 东方明珠电视塔
Dōngfāng Míngzhū Diànshìtǎ (8)
44. 东西 dōngxi (6)
45. 董事长 dǒngshìzhǎng (19)
46. 懂 dǒng (14)
47. 都 dōu (1)
48. 读 dú (5)
49. 对 duì (3)
50. 对不起 duìbuqǐ (6)
51. 对面 duìmiàn (3)
52. 顿 dùn (15)
53. 多 duō (12,15)

E

1. 二号线 èrhàoxiàn (14)

F

1. 发 fā (20)
2. 法国 Fǎguó (11)
3. 饭 fàn (7)
4. 饭店 fàndiàn (3)
5. 方便 fāngbiàn (13)
6. 房间 fángjiān (2)
7. 飞机 fēijī (11)
8. 非常 fēicháng (10)

9.	费	fèi	(18)
10.	分	fēn	(5)
11.	份	fèn	(19)
12.	封	fēng	(6)
13.	夫妇	fūfù	(8)
14.	夫人	fūrén	(8)
15.	服务	fúwù	(17)
16.	服务员	fúwùyuán	(17)
17.	父母	fùmǔ	(15)
18.	付	fù	(18)
19.	附近	fùjìn	(3)
20.	副	fù	(9)

G

1.	干杯	gānbēi	(10)
2.	干净	gānjìng	(8)
3.	感冒	gǎnmào	(4)
4.	干	gàn	(5)
5.	刚	gāng	(20)
6.	刚才	gāngcái	(17)
7.	高	gāo	(8)
8.	高尔夫	gāoěrfū	(5)
9.	高兴	gāoxìng	(10)
10.	搞	gǎo	(20)
11.	告诉	gàosu	(11)
12.	哥哥	gēge	(4)
13.	歌	gē	(19)
14.	个	gè	(4)
15.	个子	gèzi	(10)
16.	各	gè	(10)
17.	给	gěi	(9,15)
18.	跟/和/同…一样	gēn/hé/tóng…yīyàng	(10)
19.	工作	gōngzuò	(14)
20.	公共汽车	gōnggòngqìchē	(14)
21.	公司	gōngsī	(1)
22.	公寓	gōngyù	(2)
23.	顾客	gùkè	(4)
24.	管理员	guǎnlǐyuán	(2)
25.	广州	Guǎngzhōu	(9)
26.	逛	guàng	(6)
27.	贵	guì	(8,12)
28.	国宝	guóbǎo	(13)
29.	过	guò	(5,8)
30.	过	guo	(13)

H

1.	还	hái	(9)
2.	还是	háishi	(13)
3.	孩子	háizi	(16)
4.	汉语	Hànyǔ	(2)
5.	好	hǎo	(1,16,19,20)
6.	好吃	hǎochī	(8)
7.	好好儿	hǎohāor	(9)
8.	好久	hǎojiǔ	(7)
9.	好看	hǎokàn	(8)
10.	号码	hàomǎ	(18)
11.	喝	hē	(6)
12.	和	hé	(3)
13.	很	hěn	(8)
14.	红	hóng	(11)
15.	红茶	hóngchá	(6)
16.	红绿灯	hónglǜdēng	(8)
17.	护照	hùzhào	(17)
18.	话	huà	(10)
19.	淮海路	Huáihǎilù	(13)
20.	坏	huài	(17,20)
21.	欢迎	huānyíng	(15)
22.	黄	Huáng	(2)
23.	回	huí	(9,19)
24.	回来	huílái	(16)
25.	会	huì	(9,13,19)
26.	会/会议	huì/huìyì	(19)
27.	会客室	huìkèshì	(3)
28.	会议室	huìyìshì	(3)
29.	货	huò	(18)

J

1.	极了	jíle	(15)
2.	几	jǐ	(3,19)
3.	计划	jìhuà	(20)
4.	记	jì	(18)
5.	忌司	jìsī	(13)
6.	技术员	jìshùyuán	(1)
7.	寄	jì	(6)
8.	加班	jiābān	(19)
9.	家	jiā	(3,8)
10.	见	jiàn	(5,17)
11.	件	jiàn	(2)
12.	建议	jiànyì	(10)
13.	江兴	Jiāng Xìng	(1)
14.	交	jiāo	(18)
15.	交通	jiāotōng	(14)
16.	饺子	jiǎozi	(15)
17.	叫	jiào	(1,20)
18.	教室	jiàoshì	(4)
19.	街	jiē	(6)
20.	节	jié	(13)
21.	节日	jiérì	(13)
22.	杰夫	Jiéfū	(2)
23.	结婚	jiéhūn	(16)
24.	姐姐	jiějie	(4)
25.	介绍	jièshào	(15)
26.	斤	jīn	(6)
27.	今天	jīntiān	(9)
28.	今晚	jīnwǎn	(6)
29.	金茂大厦	Jīnmào Dàshà	(8)
30.	紧张	jǐnzhāng	(12)
31.	进	jìn	(9)
32.	进步	jìnbù	(10)
33.	京剧/京戏	jīngjù/jīngxì	(11)
34.	经常	jīngcháng	(5)
35.	精彩	jīngcǎi	(17)
36.	久	jiǔ	(15)
37.	酒	jiǔ	(9)
38.	就	jiù	(2,8)
39.	旧金山	Jiùjīnshān	(13)
40.	橘子	júzi	(11)
41.	句子	jùzi	(10)
42.	觉得	juéde	(10)

K

1.	咖啡馆	kāfēiguǎn	(3)
2.	卡拉OK	kǎlā'ōukèi	(13)
3.	卡森	Kǎsēn	(3)
4.	开	kāi	(9,11,19)
5.	开玩笑	kāiwánxiào	(17)
6.	看	kàn	(5)
7.	考试	kǎoshì	(14)
8.	科长	kēzhǎng	(1)
9.	咳嗽	késou	(9)
10.	可爱	kě'ài	(15)
11.	可乐	kělè	(13)
12.	可是	kěshì	(20)
13.	可以	kěyǐ	(18)
14.	刻	kè	(5)
15.	客人	kèrén	(4)
16.	课	kè	(12)
17.	课本	kèběn	(4)
18.	课文	kèwén	(5)
19.	肯德基	Kěndéjī	(11)
20.	空儿	kòngr	(4)
21.	口	kǒu	(4)
22.	块	kuài	(2,11)
23.	快	kuài	(17)
24.	快递	kuàidì	(20)
25.	快乐	kuàilè	(10)
26.	宽	kuān	(8)

L

1.	蜡烛	làzhú	(10)
2.	来	lái	(7,15,19)
3.	来不及	láibují	(20)
4.	来得及	láidejí	(19)

5. 老师 lǎoshī (1)
6. 了 le (3,7)
7. 累 lèi (13)
8. 礼物 lǐwù (7)
9. 里 li (3)
10. 力气 lìqi (12)
11. 练习 liànxí (20)
12. 两 liǎng (13)
13. 聊天儿 liáotiānr (14)
14. 林达 Líndá (2)
15. 领事馆 lǐngshìguǎn (17)
16. 留学 liúxué (16)
17. 留学生 liúxuéshēng (1)
18. 留言 liúyán (19)
19. 楼 lóu (2)
20. 楼上 lóushang (4)
21. 鲁迅公园 Lǔxùn Gōngyuán (16)
22. 鲁迅故居 Lǔxùn Gùjū (16)
23. 鲁迅纪念馆 Lǔxùn Jìniànguǎn (16)
24. 陆家嘴 Lùjiāzuǐ (8)
25. 路 lù (8)
26. 罗斯 Luósī (7)
27. 旅游 lǚyóu (7)
28. 绿 lǜ (11)

M

1. 妈妈 māma (15)
2. 麻烦 máfan (15)
3. 马路 mǎlù (8)
4. 马上 mǎshàng (7)
5. 吗 ma (1)
6. 买 mǎi (6)
7. 麦当劳 Màidāngláo (11)
8. 慢 màn (17)
9. 忙 máng (9)
10. 毛 máo (11)
11. 毛巾 máojīn (6)
12. 毛衣 máoyī (6)
13. 帽子 màozi (11)
14. 没关系 méiguānxi (12)
15. 没有 méiyǒu (4)
17. 煤气 méiqì (18)
17. 每次 měicì (18)
18. 每天 měitiān (14)
19. 美国 Měiguó (1)
20. 美容院 měiróngyuàn (6)
21. 妹妹 mèimei (15)
22. 门卫 ménwèi (7)
23. 们 men (1)
24. 秘书 mìshū (1)
25. 面包 miànbāo (12)
26. 面包店 miànbāodiàn (3)
27. 名字 míngzi (20)
28. 明白 míngbai (5)
29. 明天 míngtiān (5)
30. 明珠线 Míngzhūxiàn (14)
31. 茉莉花茶 mòlìhuāchá (6)

N

1. 拿 ná (18)
2. 哪 nǎ (2)
3. 哪里/哪儿 nǎli/nǎr (3)
4. 那 nà (4)
5. 那个 nàge (2)
6. 那里/那儿 nàli/nàr (3)
7. 那么 nàme (18)
8. 那样 nàyàng (19)
9. 男 nán (4)
10. 南京 Nánjīng (8)
11. 南京西路 Nánjīngxīlù (13)
12. 南浦大桥 Nánpǔ Dàqiáo (8)
13. 难 nán (18)
14. 呢 ne (5)
15. 能 néng (20)
16. 嗯 ǹg (14)
17. 你 nǐ (1)

18. 你看 nǐkàn (16)
19. 年纪 niánjì (11)
20. 年轻 niánqīng (12)
21. 您 nín (1)
22. 牛奶 niúnǎi (6)
23. 纽约 Niǔyuē (4)
24. 女 nǚ (4)
25. 女儿 nǚ'ér (15)

O

1. 哦 ò (5)

P

1. 排球 páiqiú (12)
2. 旁边 pángbiān (3)
3. 跑步 pǎobù (17)
4. 朋友 péngyou (3)
5. 啤酒 píjiǔ (9)
6. 便宜 piányi (8)
7. 票 piào (11)
8. 漂亮 piàoliang (8)
9. 苹果 píngguǒ (11)
10. 浦东 Pǔdōng (7)
11. 葡萄酒 pútaojiǔ (11)

Q

1. 其他 qítā (12)
2. 起床 qǐchuáng (5)
3. 汽车 qìchē (11)
4. 铅笔 qiānbǐ (2)
5. 钱 qián (16)
6. 钱包 qiánbāo (2)
7. 巧克力 qiǎokèlì (13)
8. 切 qiē (10)
9. 请 qǐng (1)
10. 请假 qǐngjià (12)
11. 请问 qǐngwèn (2)
12. 取 qǔ (17)
13. 去 qù (6)
14. 去年 qùnián (17)
15. 缺席 quēxí (12)

R

1. 然后 ránhòu (10)
2. 让 ràng (20)
3. 热 rè (8)
4. 热闹 rènao (8)
5. 热情 rèqíng (17)
6. 人 rén (1)
7. 人口 rénkǒu (19)
8. 人民广场 Rénmín Guǎngchǎng (8)
9. 认真 rènzhēn (17)
10. 软件 ruǎnjiàn (2)

S

1. 伞 sǎn (2)
2. 散步 sànbù (16)
3. 嗓子 sǎngzi (9)
4. 沙发 shāfā (4)
5. 商品 shāngpǐn (6)
6. 上 shang (4)
7. 上班 shàngbān (5)
8. 上次 shàngcì (12)
9. 上(个)月 shàng(ge)yuè (12)
10. 上海 Shànghǎi (1)
11. 上海博物馆 Shànghǎi Bówùguǎn (13)
12. 上海大剧院 Shànghǎi Dàjùyuàn (13)
13. 上海商城 Shànghǎi Shāngchéng (8)
14. 上海书城 Shànghǎi Shūchéng (13)
15. 上课 shàngkè (20)
16. 上午 shàngwǔ (5)

17.	烧烤	shāokǎo	(11)
18.	稍	shāo	(4)
19.	少	shǎo	(9)
20.	申请	shēnqǐng	(18)
21.	申请表	shēnqǐngbiǎo	(18)
22.	身体	shēntǐ	(12)
23.	什么	shénme	(1)
24.	生词	shēngcí	(20)
25.	生日	shēngri	(10)
26.	声音	shēngyīn	(19)
27.	时候	shíhou	(10)
28.	时间	shíjiān	(16)
29.	食堂	shítáng	(16)
30.	事	shì	(12)
31.	事务所	shìwùsuǒ	(3)
32.	是	shì	(1)
33.	是…的	shì…de	(17)
34.	室	shì	(2)
35.	收拾	shōushi	(20)
36.	手表	shǒubiǎo	(2)
37.	手机	shǒujī	(2)
38.	手续	shǒuxù	(17)
39.	首	shǒu	(19)
40.	售票处	shòupiàochù	(14)
41.	售票机	shòupiàojī	(14)
42.	书	shū	(2)
43.	书店	shūdiàn	(3)
44.	书架	shūjià	(4)
45.	叔叔	shūshu	(15)
46.	熟悉	shúxī	(20)
47.	双	shuāng	(15)
48.	谁	shuí	(1)
49.	水果店	shuǐguǒdiàn	(3)
50.	睡	shuì	(16)
51.	睡觉	shuìjiào	(5)
52.	顺便	shùnbiàn	(6)
53.	顺利	shùnlì	(10)
54.	说	shuō	(5)
55.	司机	sījī	(8)
56.	宋庆龄故居	Sòngqìnglíng Gùjū	(16)
57.	送	sòng	(17)
58.	岁	suì	(15)
59.	随便	suíbiàn	(10)
60.	隧道	suìdào	(8)

T

1.	他	tā	(1)
2.	她	tā	(1)
3.	太…了	tài…le	(10)
4.	太太	tàitai	(3)
5.	疼	téng	(9)
6.	天	tiān	(5)
7.	添	tiān	(15)
8.	填	tián	(18)
9.	条	tiáo	(6)
10.	听	tīng	(5)
11.	听说	tīngshuō	(16)
12.	听写	tīngxiě	(20)
13.	同事	tóngshì	(10)
14.	同意	tóngyì	(13)
15.	偷	tōu	(20)
16.	头	tóu	(9)
17.	图书馆	túshūguǎn	(3)

W

1.	哇	wa	(6)
2.	外滩	Wàitān	(6)
3.	完	wán	(16)
4.	玩儿	wánr	(7)
5.	晚饭	wǎnfàn	(13)
6.	晚上	wǎnshang	(5)
7.	碗	wǎn	(15)
8.	王丽丽	Wáng Lìli	(1)
9.	往	wǎng	(11)
10.	忘记	wàngjì	(8)
11.	位	wèi	(2)

12. 胃 wèi (9)
13. 喂 wèi (7)
14. 文文 Wénwen (15)
15. 问讯处 wènxùnchù (3)
16. 我 wǒ (1)
17. 午饭 wǔfàn (15)
18. 午觉 wǔjiào (16)

X

1. 洗 xǐ (5)
2. 洗澡 xǐzǎo (16)
3. 喜欢 xǐhuān (9)
4. 下 xià (9)
5. 下班 xiàbān (16)
6. 下面 xiàmiàn (12)
7. 下去 xiàqu (7)
8. 下午 xiàwǔ (5)
9. 下星期 xiàxīngqī (14)
10. 夏天 xiàtiān (8)
11. 先 xiān (7)
12. 先…然后… xiān…ránhòu… (20)
13. 先生 xiānsheng (1)
14. 闲 xián (19)
15. 现在 xiànzài (4)
16. 香港 Xiānggǎng (10)
17. 想 xiǎng (11)
18. 小 xiǎo (8)
19. 小姐 xiǎojie (1)
20. 林达 Líndá (2)
21. 小笼包 xiǎolóngbāo (16)
22. 校长 xiàozhǎng (1)
22. 鞋 xié (15)
23. 写 xiě (12)
24. 谢谢 xièxie (1)
25. 辛苦 xīnkǔ (19)
26. 辛苦了 xīnkǔle (20)
27. 新天地 Xīntiāndì (13)
28. 信 xìn (2)
29. 星期 xīngqī (5)
30. 星期日/星期天 xīngqīrì/xīngqītiān (5)
31. 行 xíng (19)
32. 行李 xíngli (7)
33. 姓 xìng (1)
34. 休息 xiūxi (5)
35. 徐家汇 Xújiāhuì (14)
36. 学 xué (6)
37. 学生 xuésheng (1)
38. 学习 xuéxí (5)
39. 学校 xuéxiào (3)

Y

1. 颜色 yánsè (18)
2. 杨浦大桥 Yángpǔ Dàqiáo (8)
3. 药 yào (4)
4. 要 yào (9)
5. 要是…就… yàoshì…jiù… (17)
6. 钥匙 yàoshi (2)
7. 也 yě (2)
8. 也许 yěxǔ (19)
9. 一边…一边… yībiān…yībiān… (14)
10. 一点儿 yīdiǎnr (6)
11. 一号线 yīhàoxiàn (14)
12. 一…就… yī…jiù… (16)
13. 一块儿 yīkuàir (16)
14. 一起 yīqǐ (13)
15. 一下 yīxià (4)
16. 一下儿 yīxiàr (14)
17. 衣服 yīfu (2)
18. 医生 yīshēng (4)
19. 医院 yīyuàn (4)
20. 已经 yǐjing (12)
21. 以后 yǐhòu (10)
22. 因此 yīncǐ (9)

23.	因为…	yīnwèi…	(9)
24.	音乐	yīnyuè	(13)
25.	银行	yínháng	(3)
26.	饮料	yǐnliào	(20)
27.	英语/英文	Yīngyǔ/Yīngwén	(2)
28.	用	yòng	(20)
29.	邮局	yóujú	(3)
30.	邮票	yóupiào	(11)
31.	游泳	yóuyǒng	(9)
32.	有	yǒu	(4)
33.	有趣	yǒuqù	(14)
34.	有意思	yǒuyìsi	(12)
35.	又…又…	yòu…yòu…	(8)
36.	右面	yòumiàn	(3)
37.	雨	yǔ	(9)
38.	玉佛寺	Yùfósì	(16)
39.	豫园	Yùyuán	(13)
40.	约	yuē	(19)
41.	约翰·史密斯	Yuēhàn Shǐmìsī	(1)

Z

1.	杂技	zájì	(11)
2.	杂志	zázhì	(7)
3.	再	zài	(12,16)
4.	在	zài	(3,7)
5.	咱们	zánmen	(13)
6.	脏	zāng	(8)
7.	糟糕	zāogāo	(17)
8.	早	zǎo	(19)
9.	早饭	zǎofàn	(19)
10.	早上	zǎoshang	(5)
11.	怎么	zěnme	(5,19)
12.	怎么样	zěnmeyàng	(7)
13.	展览	zhǎnlǎn	(13)
14.	张	zhāng	(2)
15.	张颖	Zhāng Yǐng	(1)
16.	账单	zhàngdān	(18)
17.	着急	zháojí	(17)
18.	找	zhǎo	(7,17)
19.	这	zhè	(2)
20.	这个	zhège	(2)
21.	这里/这儿	zhèli/zhèr	(3)
22.	这么	zhème	(10)
23.	真	zhēn	(8)
24.	真的	zhēnde	(12)
25.	正常	zhèngcháng	(20)
26.	正在	zhèngzài	(7)
27.	支	zhī	(2)
28.	知道	zhīdào	(3)
29.	职员	zhíyuán	(1)
30.	只	zhǐ	(14)
31.	只好	zhǐhǎo	(18)
32.	纸	zhǐ	(20)
33.	中国	Zhōngguó	(1)
34.	中药	zhōngyào	(9)
35.	种	zhǒng	(11)
36.	周	Zhōu	(2)
37.	驻外人员	zhùwàirényuán	(1)
38.	祝	zhù	(10)
39.	《祝你生日快乐》	《Zhùnǐ shēngri kuàilè》	(10)
40.	抓紧	zhuājǐn	(12)
41.	桌子	zhuōzi	(4)
42.	字	zì	(12)
43.	自动	zìdòng	(14)
44.	自己	zìjǐ	(8)
45.	自来水	zìláishuǐ	(18)
46.	自行车	zìxíngchē	(19)
47.	总公司	zǒnggōngsī	(4)
48.	总经理	zǒngjīnglǐ	(1)
49.	走	zǒu	(15)
50.	昨天	zuótiān	(9)
51.	昨晚	zuówǎn	(20)
52.	左面	zuǒmiàn	(3)
53.	左右	zuǒyòu	(5)

54.	作业	zuòyè	(12)	57.	做	zuò	(7)
55.	作用	zuòyòng	(9)	58.	做客	zuòkè	(15)
56.	坐	zuò	(1,14)				

图书在版编目(C I P)数据

一见钟情学汉语:英语版:初级. 上 / 施洁民等编著;范祥涛译.
—上海:上海译文出版社,2009.9
ISBN 978-7-5327-4871-6

I.一… II.①施…②范… III.汉语—对外汉语教学—教材
IV.H195.4

中国版本图书馆CIP数据核字(2009)第124122号

Love Chinese at First Sight

(***Primary Level I***)

一见钟情学汉语(初级上)

(英语版)

施洁民 [日]蒲丰彦 编著

范祥涛 译

上海世纪出版股份有限公司
译文出版社出版、发行
网址:www.yiwen.com.cn
200001 上海福建中路193号 www.ewen.cc
全国新华书店经销
上海市印刷七厂有限公司印刷

开本890×1240 1/32 印张6.25 插页3 字数186,000
2009年9月第1版 2009年9月第1次印刷
印数:0,001—3,000册
ISBN 978-7-5327-4871-6/H·913
定价:39.00元
(含MP3一张)

如有质量问题,请与承印厂质量科联系。T:021-69113557